First American Printing

This publication was made possible thanks in part to the generous support of the Andrew W. Mellon Foundation, and our individual contributors.

ISBN: 0-934257-69-8

Published by Story Line Press
Three Oaks Farm
Brownsville, OR
97327-9718

Book design by Lysa McDowell

ACKNOWLEDGEMENTS

The author wishes to thank the editors of the follow-
ing reviews, in which some of these stories first appeared:
*Ambergris, Amelia, Asylum, Dekalb Literary Arts Journal,
Fiction Forum, Habersham Review, Negative Capability, The
Paper Bag, The Paterson Literary Review, Truly Fine, Un-
knowns.*

"Every Now and Then," "No One Else but Myself,"
"When there is no Ending," "Turning the Page," "Morning
Coffee," "The Identity Bracelet," "My Mother's Slate"
and "The Fond Memory" were first published together—
under the title *Apperceptions*—in the *South Dakota Review* (Summer, 1989). "The View from the Upper Window" was published in the same issue. *The Apperceptions* were reprinted in 1990, in the form of a broadside,
for the Festival de la Nouvelle in Saint-Quentin, France.
"What I Knew about Anna" appeared as a broadside at
the 1989 Festival de la Nouvelle.

"Sally" was first published in 15 newspapers of the
London Newspaper Group (on May 7, 1987), as the winner
of one of the weekly London Newspaper Group / Mont
Blanc Gold Pen Awards. It was later reprinted in *Paris
Transcontinental* (Spring, 1990).

"Cody" first appeared in *Imaginary Friends*, an anthology
(Stacyville, Iowa: Peak Output Unlimited, 1989).

"The Doctors' Club" first appeared in *A Celebration of
Libraries*, an anthology published by Doubleday in 1990.

I.   TOWER PARK

II.   THE VIEW FROM
THE UPPER WINDOW

for Nature

&

for my father

I. TOWER PARK

My first death was Bud, Nancy's father. He was a round, bald-headed man who loved fishing and barbecued steaks. Often he had me and Nancy hop into the T-Bird convertibles he drove home—he sold cars for one of the Ford dealers—and back down the driveway we would go for a spin up and down Urbandale Avenue. Bud had his own special smell, the smell of profuse sweating and after-shave lotion. He had a ruddy face, a stout nose, and short, chubby fingers.

His heart stopped out in the middle of a remote Minnesota lake. Doris Jean and Nancy struggled with the outboard motor; eventually they managed to start it; they raced across the flat water; by the time they reached the shore he was dead. Forty-three years old. Someone came along by chance and helped them lug the corpse up the bank.

When the news was telephoned around the neighborhood, my father told me to go over to Nancy's and talk with her.

"But I don't know what to say," I replied.

"You'll find the words," said my father.

My mother looked up from the casserole she was preparing for Doris Jean, and added:

"It's something everyone needs to learn how to do."

Instead of taking the shortcut through Ruth and Ernie's backyard, I took the long way around to Nancy's: down 48th Street to Snyder Drive, then back up 48th Street Place to her house. When I arrived, she and several of

3

her girlfriends were talking out on the front steps. Nancy got up and led me back across the lawn. We sat down in the grass near the sidewalk.

"Oh Johnny," she sighed, "you don't have to say anything."

She then recounted the latest practical joke which they had played on the O'Connell sisters.

"The police really did show up," she laughed. "But by that time we had turned off every light in the house. How could they have proved it was us, anyway?"

After the story a silence fell between us. In a moment I got up and said:

"I feel really bad about your father, Nancy."

Nancy shrugged her shoulders, her lips pursed, her eyes downcast and watery.

"Thanks for coming over, Johnny."

The funeral took place the next day at the Methodist Church. I had never seen a dead man before. Bud's waxy face, his dapper black suit, the red carnation in his lapel—I can't say that I was shocked. His eyes were closed. Not a muscle twitched. His double chin seemed molded of clay. I observed Bud with a gentle, uncommitted curiosity, as many years later I would, from afar, observe street scenes in foreign capitals. Then my mother pushed me out of the church and I overheard her whispering to my father:

"I hate open caskets."

A rather similar sort of gentle detachment I sought to maintain when, nearly twenty years after Bud's death, I found myself back from Europe standing at the funeral home in front of my mother's casket. There she was, just as I had known and loved her, wearing her navy-blue suit. On her wrist was her charm bracelet and in her hands she cupped a red and pink nosegay.

I put my hand on her brow and caressed it lightly with the tips of my fingers. Then I touched her cheek with the back of my hand. The skin had no resilience. The embalming chemicals had worked: her face was as hard as stone.

I turned away and found a chair. I only remember a dull, numbed sensation while sitting there, a sort of unbreathing, tepid dreariness both within me and without. Nothing stirred. The contours of my body had blended with the mournfulness of death, with the musty perfume of the flowers, with the sheen of burnished surfaces. Then someone said something to me and I shooed the words away, but when I looked up I saw there was no one and immediately remembered Nancy, my childhood playmate, and imagined her arm around me in consolation.

"Now it's my turn," she said. "You'll get over it."

I sat there a while longer looking over at the door, then I took a deep breath, got up, cleared a path with my hands through everything that was hovering thick and heavy in front of me and walked out to my car in the parking lot.

It was only many years later, after Ernie's funeral, that I learned that he and Ruth were never married.

"His wife was a Catholic and wouldn't give him a divorce," explained my mother.

"You mean that for twenty years he came over every evening after work?"

"That's what he did," she replied.

She changed the subject. My mother disapproved of the relationship and had doubts about Ernie's integrity. For us kids, though, Ernie was generous and noble. When we were small he would hold us on his knee. On summer evenings Ruth and Ernie sat out in their backyard, and it was there that we usually played.

"Hey little Pete!" he would cry. "Come on over here."

Little Peter Meert would run over to Ernie's side.

"That was a great catch you made," he would say, reaching for the baseball, weighing it in his hand, then tossing it back.

When I was nine or ten, I began earning money after school in the winter by shoveling the snow off Ruth and Ernie's driveway.

"Finished?" Ernie would ask in his hoarse voice, inspecting it. "Now make Ruth real happy and clear a path out to the garbage cans."

The cans stood behind the garage. When I knocked on the door five minutes later, Ernie would open it and hand me two, sometimes three times the usual amount.

The same was true during the summer, when on Saturdays

I washed their cars for a dollar each. As I was rinsing them off, Ernie would arrive with his chammy cloth, showing me how to polish the chrome. No one else in the neighborhood had one of those: we all used old bath towels. The work was arduous; the chammy stuck to the shiny metal; in the end Ernie not only rewarded me with money but cracked jokes as if I were an adult.

What displeased my mother and the other women in the neighborhood was Ernie's alcoholism. But his was not the dull-eyed, driveling kind, rather a need to drink which turned him jovial and carefree. I have no recollection of Ernie without a gin in one hand and a Camel cigarette in the other. He walked around the backyard like that, examining Ruth's few flowers, or simply sat there with her, on folding lawn chairs, and enjoyed the sunset. It was through their backyard that we cut whenever going over to 48th Street Place, where Nancy, Steve, the O'Connell sisters and the Bell brothers lived. Everyone else had closed off their lawns with fences and hedges. Ruth and Ernie had a hedge, but they let us keep open a hole through which we could crawl. We wore out the grass; we broke off branches for whips; one of the privet bushes died. But Ruth and Ernie didn't mind. Ruth didn't have time to care for a nice lawn and garden; she was the only woman in the neighborhood who worked.

Her husband had died young. He had worked in the Tax Department with Ernie, who had been his best friend. What caused a sensation in the neighborhood one Halloween Eve was when Senator Bob Whitman came over to Ruth and Ernie's. It was my sister Joan who told me, but by that time I was already in high school.

Ruth was a tall, stately woman who wore nicely tailored

tweed suits and had her glossy blond hair piled high on the back of her head in a bun. I associated her with the French. She spoke slowly, with a slight Eastern sonority to her pronunciation, and was at times as solemn as Ernie was gregarious. Not once did she take a vacation. Every single day of the year, from five o'clock on, Ruth and Ernie were inseparable.

During the summer, late at night, sometimes my mother sent me out to the back porch to retrieve her ice-tea glass or her sewing. Through the screen window I would then perceive the far-off red glow of Ernie's cigarette, rising slowly to his mouth, descending. They were still out there talking; we had left them over an hour ago.

Eventually my mother would come out on the back porch to see what I was doing. Into the house she would usher me, jerking from my hand the glass or sewing, pushing me off to the bathroom to brush my teeth.

Later, in bed, in the not quite total darkness, I wouldn't be able to get Ruth and Ernie out of my mind. What were they talking about? Earlier that evening Ernie had been so full of mirth, wisecracking, rattling the ice in his glass; Ruth too had been laughing, her head tossed back, her face pale and gentle.... Now all was shadow, the crickets were screeching, the air was damp and cool and motionless. I would feel saddened and bewildered, as if their backyard conversations so late at night revealed or foreboded something I needed to discern.

Goodwin's corporal and intellectual capabilities were once summed up by Mr. Wilson, my tenth-grade geometry teacher, who said:

"He's a mental genius and a physical moron."

By then Goodwin had surpassed in learning all his classmates and teachers, but still had clinging to his bones the blubber of his infancy, the first child of Merle Craig, nuclear engineer, and his wife Margaret, a fretting, cross-eyed woman who had studied chemistry and mathematics. The Craigs lived only four houses to the south of us, past Ruth and Ernie's house, past the Meert's and the Manson's.

So Goodwin was one of my first playmates. I remember my mother walking me down to their house, her talking with Mrs. Craig out in their front lawn, then after a while that she wouldn't accompany me anymore. I was still allowed to go, but would hear her saying things to my father like:

"She's going to make a sissy out of that boy!"

It is true, at Goodwin's we never played catch, raced, or climbed trees. At a very early age he had Erector Sets and microscopes, butterfly nets and formaldehyde, dissecting kits and telescopes. It was Goodwin who showed me how to set a piece of toilet paper on fire by concentrating rays of sunlight through a magnifying glass.

We were thus companions not very long. His mother would put my baseballs and basketballs in the hall closet whenever I came over; I never could follow the bubbling liquids in Goodwin's alembics. He was such a gentle, harmless boy, ever distracted by the brute facts of the world but never by its cares, roly-poly like the joyous Buddha, with a big fat belly and a gaping belly button, with breasts, with buttocks that wobbled and wiggled. Every Saturday morning Mr. Craig trimmed Goodwin's blond hair into a butch crewcut. After I stopped playing with him, Goodwin would sit by himself in their front yard, examining the blades of grass and the bugs.

He was like that at school as well. During recess Goodwin would wander off into the adjoining field, talking to himself and picking up things. Often he brought back grasshoppers or worms or tiny tree frogs. The girls would scream; someone would pry Goodwin's hand back open, snatch whatever it was and throw it out the window; Mrs. Lawrence would threaten.... But she never did send Goodwin to the principal's office. How could she punish a boy so pathetically defenseless and alone?

Such antics, which Goodwin continued to perform long into our high-school years, were just one of the reasons why our teachers dreaded his presence in their classrooms, though he was by far their best pupil. Gym instructors had to find activities for him while the rest of us were climbing ropes or playing dodgeball. Sometimes, amused by some private thought, Goodwin burst out giggling in the middle of class, loudly and uncontrollably. In his high-pitched, nasal voice he interrupted teachers with irrelevant remarks. Then, expatiating upon one of those abstruse subjects about which only he was informed, he would send the entire class into an uproar.

Such was the consequence of the analogy he drew with the "Wheatstone Bridge." We looked around the classroom at each other while Goodwin, lecturing away, waddled to the blackboard and drew diagrams and scribbled figures. Some of the sketches did look like bridges and he seemed to be talking, as Mrs. Lawrence had been, about the Civil War, about the Battle of Bull Run. One by one we realized that he was talking about electricity. The snickering, starting at diverse tables, soon blended into a chorus of unrestrained laughter.

It was Mrs. Lawrence's habit to say nothing on such occasions, just to stand there calmly staring at us, her arms folded across her chest. When the laughing dwindled to a tense silence, she sneered icily:

"Well, now you can all put your heads down until four o'clock."

Goodwin, as if violently shaken awake, plodded heavily back to his seat.

"Not you, Goodwin," she commanded. "You go home. You're dismissed."

I watched Goodwin out of the corner of my eye, my head already down against the warm varnished wood of my desk. He looked unbelievingly at Mrs. Lawrence for a long moment; there were round tears in his eyes; then he continued on his way as if nothing had been said, sat down, and like the rest of us folded his arms in front of him and put his head down on his desk.

Back then we said that Mrs. Shelley was senile, but from the distance of years I think that my father should have gone ahead and cut down the hedge. On the other side were flowers which, before the hedge grew, had basked in the afternoon sun. Mrs. Shelley would rap on the front door; that evening my father would get out the shears and trim the privet down about five inches; the next afternoon at three Mrs. Shelley would be out there with her ruler to measure the shadow. We had let the privet grow since Mrs. Shelley sat at her kitchen window and spied on our backyard and porch.

But generally we were on good terms with her. Every Thanksgiving we invited her over for dinner.

"No, thank you," she would say when my mother passed the dressing. "I hate dressing."

"No, just give me a glass of lukewarm water."

"I'll only take a sliver. I ate before coming."

Every year comments such as those made Ann, Joan and me crack up behind our hands and my mother vow never to invite her over again. Mrs. Shelley could have, however, that embarrassing yet cuddlesome charm of an obese grandmother, one who at the lowest ebb of our affection for her knows how to bring over a plate of orange rolls or to appear, ready to be taken shopping, all powdered and perfumed and clutching a dark-blue purse covered with infinitesimal black beads.

Mrs. Shelley wore gloves whenever she was out, which was usually to Tobey's Grocery Store or to one of the frequent meetings of the Women's Prayer Group. She also belonged to various bridge clubs, and thus her days were spent.

But then her friends began dying, one after another. About that time her son Bill was transferred to Kansas City. Despite the easy drive, only rarely did he come up with his family to visit her. It was during those years that Mrs. Shelley, seeing us playing one day out in our front lawn, called us over and asked us to call her "Nana."

She also expanded her garden, considerably. A bed of variously colored roses composed the center of it; around them grew marigolds and ageratums and daisies and other common flowers, but all in unusual hues. Flowers bordered her driveway. Along the back of her house sprouted the rarer, more fragile species, the seeds and bulbs for which she ordered out of catalogs from nurseries in Oregon and Pennsylvania.

All morning long, then again in the evening, Nana hoed and weeded and planted in her garden. From the upstairs hall window I sometimes watched her— wearing her long dark-blue workdress and her stiff sunbonnet, poking and scratching and shoving at the dirt with her oaken-handled tools, her upper arms flabby and wobbly as she stabbed away, her will stubborn and steadfast and persevering. Her garden was immaculate, weedless, geometric; the teeth of the narrow rake left straight little furrows between each row of roses; every morning, after she had watered the evening before, she raked the rows out again. But who ever saw that garden besides us and the Farnys, who lived next door to her on the other side?

It is true that Nana, even at that point, had become a little senile. When later we moved to another neighborhood (when I was fifteen), we would hear from the old neighbors we occasionally ran into at the shopping center, that Nana had been telephoning again, asking the men over to shine a flashlight into the corners of her closets. Her garden she eventually abandoned; the weeds choked out the marigolds and ageratums; one day workers from the city came and sawed down her enormous shade trees, which like all the other elms in the neighborhood had caught the Dutch elm disease. Then a year or two later Nana had a stroke, and that was the last time I saw her: at the hospital.

She recovered and lived two or three more years. I was in Des Moines that summer when she died, but I didn't go to the funeral.

"There were only eight of us," said my mother when she came home. "Young Bill asked about you."

She was referring to William Shelley III, Nana's grandson.

"What's he up to these days?" I asked.

"Oh, he works in a shoestore or something like that."

I went out of the kitchen and on upstairs, shutting my bedroom door behind me.

And there I sat for a while, knowing I would be late but remembering Mrs. Shelley, Nana, her loneliness and her perseverance, and the immaculate, geometric garden that so few of us in the old neighborhood ever even saw.

One day when I was ten years old, walking home from school alone, I bent over, scooped up a handful of snow, packed it into an icy ball, threw it as hard as I could against the side of a passing taxicab. The driver slammed on the brakes, the car skidded, stopped. The driver jumped out, chased me down the median of Urbandale Avenue to 46th Street. I was running for my life. He caught up with me. He grabbed my parka, spun me round, shoved me down into the snow, rubbed my face in it. Then he dragged me all the way back to his cab. He threw me against the side; threatening to slap me he demanded my name and address. Then he pushed me, away, hopped into his cab. Through my tears I saw him writing something. Rolling down his window, he yelled:

"Have fun with the Police, fucker!"

He drove off with a loud whirr, his wheels spinning. When I got home, my eyes rimming with tears, I told my mother I had been beaten up by some Catholic kids from Holy Trinity.

Nothing happened until Christmas, a few days later. My parents gave me a new bicycle. There it was when I came downstairs, near the tree, leaning against an armchair. It was black and wound with blue ribbons.

"The Police Station should be open tomorrow," said my father as I was undoing them. "We'll have to go down for a license."

I kept undoing the ribbons, my eyes turned away, my mouth open, unable to swallow.

Several days later I found myself in the car, gripping the armrest, wondering whether I ought to tell my father the truth. We were speeding down Keosauqua Way, through the Black neighborhood. The city had been clearing ground there for the new expressway. I looked out at what had become a vacant field, slate gray and frozen.

"What's going to happen?" I thought.

A tall, lanky sergeant with an oblong face and bristly white hair met us in the lobby, shook my father's hand, then mine, squatted down in front of me. He looked me straight in the eye. I held my breath.

He started talking about bicycle safety rules. He asked me if I knew the arm signals. He checked the bell and light. He made sure I had put a reflector on the back fender. Then he wanted to see my lock and warned me about bicycle thieves.

"Riding double is illegal," he added.

"John's a serious young man," interjected my father.

At last the sergeant had me fill in a form and gave me the tin license plate.

"But why didn't you tell us?" exclaimed my mother when years later I told her what had happened. "We would have defended you."

I chuckled, my mother shook her head in disbelief, I poured us each a second cup of coffee. Then she picked up her napkin, dabbed it lightly round the corners of her mouth. She sighed, reached for her cigarettes.

As she was fumbling in her purse I saw her face clouding.

Neither of us said anything for a while; the silence was painful, awkward; then the subject was changed.

My first obstacle in life, at least the first of which I was fully conscious, was that spillway at Springbrook State Park. It was a concrete structure, slimy and scum-covered, which rose abruptly at an angle. Viscous water trickled down over its entire surface. The air sat heavy upon it, misty, dank and cold.

Mr. Ryder and his two sons, both older than I was, started moving up the spillway. Spreading their arms out like tightrope walkers, they took one trembling step after another.

Then my father began mounting the spillway.

I alone lingered behind, unable to take a first step. Every time I poised my foot, my courage waned. When I looked up for the others only the slick, blank face of the spillway loomed ahead.

My father turned and made his way back down to help me.

And that is all I remember about my first obstacle in life. I know that afterwards we ate dinner around a campfire. I know that the next day the Ryder boys and I played catch. Later we stood on a small wooden bridge and threw rocks at water skippers. Then there was the tent to take down and the car to pack.

Did my father and I find a path around the spillway? Did we go back down the riverbed to where we could climb the bank? Or did I grit my teeth and, on all fours, make it to the top?

My father called the other day and after all these years I finally asked him.

He said that I had walked right up the spillway. One of the Ryder boys had slipped and fallen, but the spillway hadn't been very steep.

Why is it then that this childhood memory of difficulty and failure, in fact a figment of my imagination, comes back now and then to torment me, so much so that I lose all confidence in myself?

I have never read the short stories of George Bernard Shaw, which a foreign friend said my own recall. But in the old house a shelf of the basement bookcase held numerous works by Shaw, books having belonged to a distant cousin, Leon Hook, then to his mother, then to my paternal grandmother. Often I leafed through Shaw's books, began to read some of them, but never did find one which interested me long enough to finish it.

A few years before my grandmother died, the books by Shaw arrived, along with other sets, of Oliver Wendell Holmes, of Herbert Spencer, of Ralph Waldo Emerson. Thomas Carlyle and Lord Macauley had been among my cousin's favorite authors; there were several works translated from the German. Out in the garage my father and I built the bookcase, then painted it the shade of blue which my mother picked out for us.

Those cardboard boxes contained no surprises. The Egyptian wooden chest which we inherited at the same time told only my grandmother's tale: that Leon Hook had bought it in Cairo on his way home from India.

"From India?" I asked.

"I think so," replied my grandmother.

Leon Hook had been to India, to Hong Kong, several times to South America. That stone, imitation Aztec calender which stood on a shelf in my grandparents' living room must also have been Leon Hook's, but when my grandmother gave it to me for my birthday I forgot to ask her.

"He only worked six months a year," she would say. "Traveling."

"And the other six months?"

"I suppose he read books," she replied.

If Leon Hook wrote poetry or kept a diary, nothing has been saved. My grandmother had a few photographs: briar pipe in hand, bushy hair combed back, his head turned to the side, his eyes gazing out an invisible window. He had studied at Harvard—philosophy, thought some; others, that it had been one of the natural sciences.

"I remember his beetle and butterfly collections," said my grandmother. "After the war Aunt Nina must have misplaced them. As you know, she never recovered."

Somewhere in Europe Leon Hook, thirty-one years old, came ashore, fell victim to the influenza epidemic.

"You can imagine," my father once said, "the distress his death must have caused in the family. The women all worshipped him."

Then he pointed to the bookcase and said: "A lot of the books have uncut pages."

I sat there a long while after my father had gone upstairs.

Only later did I feel how chilly it was, the close, damp air, the footsteps overhead, the hum of the humidifier in the next room.

The story my mother would tell me about the iron-rail fence around Tower Park—that a young boy climbing it had empaled himself on one of the spikes at the top and bled to death—probably had more moral to it than truth. From my earliest recollections there was an easy way into the park—on the south side where a bar had been sawed out and where the bars on each side of the space had somehow been pried further apart—so there was no need to climb the fence, which indeed was high, slippery and without footholds. I in any case never saw anyone climb it, and if from time to time I myself took hold of the bars and stepped onto the lower horizontal rail, then peered upwards at the spikes looming black against the drifting clouds, it was only to sense shivering through me the awe of knowing I was myself, that it was I who gripped the bars, I who perceived the pain and death awaiting me.

"Climb it!" would taunt Peter or Dave, standing aside. "I dare you!"

No one in the neighborhood knew what the mushroom-shaped water tower inside the park was for, whether the water we drank every day emanated from it. Mr. Manson said that it was used for storing water, in case of an emergency.

"What sort of emergency?" I asked him.

"In case of a war," he replied. "The water will taste like hell but you'll be glad to drink it."

Mr. Manson had fought in Normandy and kept in his bedroom closet a shoebox full of cartridges, shrapnel, and bits and pieces of foreign uniforms.

But my father said the water tower was simply too expensive to tear down.

We kids didn't know what to think. At the base of the tower there was a rusty metal door, padlocked like the main gate, and we held several theories about what lay behind it. Would water rush out if the door were opened? Was there some sort of prison inside? Did someone live there? Eventually Peter tried the door; the long padlock shackle let him get it open about a half-inch; when we shined the beam of the flashlight in, the light only reflected dully against the iron of the inside trim. We placed our mouths to the crack and shouted. The hollow reverberations of our cries seemed to indicate distance. We shouted again. And again. Then we grew silent, looked at each other, and moved on.

Until I was nine or ten Tower Park was by my mother's orders off-limits, my territory extending from 49th Street to 44th Street, from Urbandale Avenue to Hickman Road. But our junior high school was located at the corner of 48th Street and Franklin Avenue, next to Tower Park. The school playground ran up to the iron-rail fence. Every day I walked home alongside the eastern edge.

Even then, when I was twelve, thirteen, fourteen years old, Tower Park remained charged with peril and adventure, both imagined and real. Sometimes at night, or early in the morning, policemen were seen patrolling the grounds. When at fourteen Janet Madler gave birth to her child, it was said that the conception had taken place under the lilac bushes of the southwest corner. And who had sawed out the missing bar? Why hadn't it ever been replaced? Who had pried apart the two alongside it? On one of our explorations in Tower Park we found a stash of firecrackers, which were prohibited in Iowa.

It was inside Tower Park that most of the after-school fights took place. Sometimes a hundred boys squeezed through the opening to watch Steve Leeman and Jon Kellens slug it out, or Rich Robbins and Mike Harrow. No teacher or principal or boy's adviser could do anything about the fights—since Tower Park was off school property—and I remember our spaniel-eyed algebra teacher, Mr. Soyer, Jeannie's father, shaking his head as he ambled by, just a few days before he died of a heart attack. The funeral procession went back up 48th Street, past Tower Park, past our junior high school where he had taught for twenty-five years, to Glendale Cemetery.

My own mother is buried in Glendale Cemetery, and it was during her funeral procession that I saw Tower Park for the last time. The iron-rail fence had been removed, as well as most of the lilac bushes. Our school playground now ran up nearly to the base of the water tower. Where we used to prowl and hide, a young boy was throwing sticks, his German shepherd bolting after them.

"The First Federated Church has bought all the land," explained my father. "Your old baseball diamond has become a parking lot. The school is closed."

Our driver suddenly accelerated. A policeman was directing traffic, whistling, waving us through.

I looked over my shoulder.

The water tower.

The boy had stopped playing with his dog. He had raised his hand to his brow as a shield against the sun and was watching our long, headlighted procession.

Sometimes while riding in the Métro I think of Cody. About her reading the newspaper in the subway—about her having to fold it in two twice—just one of her New York City stories. On she would go about the way of life there, the commuting, the cockroaches, the lunatics, the neighborhoods you couldn't walk through, Grand Central Station, many sights, more often the misery. Her husband had died young, then out west she had moved with her three children. But why Des Moines? I don't think even my parents knew. Cody had no relatives in Des Moines, but she did find a job.

She worked at Elsie's Gift Shop and in the evenings babysat for the young couples in the neighborhood. My mother used to say how courageous Cody was, but only much later, when she moved to California, did I realize how poor she had been, how hard she had worked. She lived in one of the tiniest houses in the area, at the bottom of 49th Street, behind Tobey's Grocery Store. I was rarely in that house, white, wooden, just a couple of rooms, in fact only on Halloween Eves when my father would walk us over there. When at Christmas my mother (actually my father) made pralines or peppermint ice cream, we always went to Cody's first. Cody would have her sugar cookies ready. On her front steps we would exchange our presents, our wishes for the New Year, then my father would say:

"We'd better get moving. I'll be back around seven."

During the Christmas holidays, with my parents invited to so many parties, Cody sometimes babysat for us several nights in a row.

When Cody wasn't babysitting she always seemed to be working at Elsie's, open six days a week from ten until seven. Sometimes my father picked her up there; on those occasions my mother would already have prepared the dinner, something to heat up, something tastier than our regular meals. Cody would pick at her food, telling us stories, making sure we ate all the vegetables.

Elsie's Gift Shop was located on Beaver Avenue, at the heart of the Beaverdale shopping district, eight blocks up Urbandale Avenue from our neighborhood. Next door to Elsie's was Bond's, the men's clothing store; across the alley Tom's Barber Shop and Dan's Hardware; across the street Reed's Ice Cream Shop, Jerry's Shoes, Clayton's Five-and-Dime. Until Merle Hay Plaza was built, in the far corner of northwest Des Moines (at the time a cornfield), nearly all our shopping was done in Beaverdale. Iltis Lumber Company, George's Super Valu, even the northwest branch of the Des Moines Public Library was there, a hole-in-the-wall which ten years later became "The Rice Bowl," a Chinese restaurant.

Cody clerked at Elsie's, selling glass figurines, vases, a set of dishes now and then, lots of greeting cards. Often my mother took me on her errands to Beaverdale, and we never failed to at least wave at Cody from the street. Usually we dropped in and browsed.

"Don't touch anything," my mother would warn while Cody, slipping her thin hand between the desk and Mrs. Elsie's stomach—Mrs. Elsie was ever at work on the books—would try to get into the drawer for a piece of candy. The hidden candy was reserved for the well-behaved children of regular customers.

My mother always bought something, at least a card. Perhaps she felt that by buying something she was helping Cody out. From Elsie's came our Advent calendars, came the cutouts with which we decorated our windows at Thanksgiving and Halloween, came the invitations to Joan's unforgettable family parties, came most of the demi-tasse spoons in Ann's collection. It was at Elsie's that we sat while a very old lady delicately scissored our silhouettes from a piece of black paper. Cody helped my mother pick out three matching oval frames. For years our silhouettes hung, in the old house, above the love seat in the living room.

Cody's gentle manner encouraged respect and most of the time Ann, Joan and I behaved ourselves. There was something foreign about Cody, perhaps her crisp, yet soft voice; she had by no means the gregariousness of a Midwesterner. Once, Ann emptied out the cereal boxes on the kitchen floor, but all Cody did was to tell our parents. "Co-o-o-o-dy!" Ann and Joan would cry when I was mistreating them; usually Cody had only to appear in the room and I would apologize immediately. One day I realized that her name was "Mrs." Cody. But when that evening I greeted her as "Mrs. Cody," she laughed and turned to my mother:

"Remember how hard it was for him to learn to say my name at all?"

I never called her "Cody" again.

Cody would sit on the far end of the couch in the den, sewing, reading a magazine or writing a long letter to her daughter Pat, who had graduated from nursing school, married (Ann and Joan were the flower girls) and moved to California. Cody often said that Pat was "not just any nurse," but a surgical nurse, and "not just any surgical nurse," but one specialized in eye surgery.

"You mean they cut eyes open?" I asked, wondering how that could be possible.

Cody told us of the great operations at which Pat had been present, sometimes reading aloud her daughter's equally long letters, but I only imagined horrible scenes which to this day reappear, especially whenever I recall that several of my direct ascendants have had cataract operations. I did not always pay attention to Cody. Often she was a mere presence, leaving me to my games and playmates, escorting me to bed to make sure I turned out all the lights. She let me watch the Friday-night television shows that my mother wouldn't, *The Twilight Zone* and *The Untouchables*. She let Ann and Joan put up her hair in curlers.

Then we were too old to have a babysitter. Then we moved away.

One November we received an early Christmas card from California.

"I've moved!" Cody had written in her fine hand. "It's gorgeous here! Greetings to everyone!"

The cards came only two or three Christmases more.

Cody was still alive as late as four years after that—my father ran into Tim, her son, who had returned to Des Moines to work.

"Tim said she's fine," reported my father at dinner. "But they did have to put her in a nursing home."

In a moment he added:

"I told Tim to say hello from all of us."

"What's Tim doing?" I asked.

Late that evening, from my bedroom upstairs, I heard

my mother typing in the kitchen. I went down to see what she was doing. Only the far light was on, just over the table. She had her box of stationery out.

"Who are you typing that letter to, Mom," I asked. "Grandma?"

As if gently shaken from a daydream, my mother looked up at me.

She took off her glasses.

"No, I'm writing a letter to Mrs. Cody," she replied.

I was in my old high school in Des Moines. I was walking down the long corridor which led to the junior high, Meredith Junior High. At the end of the corridor I came across a Métro station, one of those old-fashioned entryways with Art Nouveau decorations, and walked down the stairs. A few people were about. On the platform, waiting for the subway, I touched something and a piece of chewing gum stuck to my finger. I tried to rub the gum off on the side of a litter basket; as I was twisting and turning my finger I looked up; Billy Bowers was observing me.

"Billy!" I said. "It's been such a long time!"

Billy pronounced my name in a tone of voice that made our encounter seem both natural and expected.

He seemed to have gained confidence in himself.

He spoke about his sister. She was going to marry for the second time, an older man who had divorced and had three children. She was a veterinarian.

I watched him talking. Only his skin had aged, brittle, translucent like parchment. He parted his blond hair on the side, still wore blue jeans, a white T-shirt that made his upper arms look so skinny. Now he shaved; dark pinpoints of shaved stubble covered his cheeks and chin. I asked:

"Billy, do you still live with your parents?"

(It was a family joke that after graduating from high school Billy Bowers lived at home, neither working nor going on to college.)

At that Billy disappeared, but his presence lingered, an emotion, invisible. I thought:

"After all these years I've hurt Billy Bowers's feelings again."

The bus stopped at the corner of 48th Street and Urbandale Avenue.

I got off, walked up the hill and woke up.

DAVE

I don't know why, but of all my childhood playmates it is Dave I remember the least. Yet he was my companion of summer mornings. On many an after-school evening we played army, shot his slingshot. When Jimmy Cellini set fire to our garage, it was Dave who saw the smoke first, who came running to pound on our door.

I remember things we did, things we must have done, but not what Dave looked like. Was he taller than I was? I think he was. He was a year older. Skinny? Freckled? When I recall him he stands at a distance, wearing a pair of maroon jeans with white stitching. A crewcut? Light-brown eyelashes? Details present themselves—a plaid shirt, a white T-shirt—others recede, vanish. I reach out my hand to Dave, I take a step forward; the distance between us remains the same.

I sometimes think of Dave when I think of my mother, the day she slammed the front door behind me when all I had asked was to play with him; not a word was said; her eyes looked elsewhere, her head turned to the side, a curtain drawn across her face.

It is the emotion afterwards which recurs.

Dave, toys in hand, awaiting; the beads of dew springing to my shoes; in the elm across the street the sun.

There are mornings when I go through the motions of pleasure, abstracted from the present by an urgent, terrifying expectancy.

Until yesterday I had even forgotten about Andy Bill's suicide (by driving a nail into his jugular vein), which occurred a few years after his family had moved away. When my father announced that news at suppertime we realized we had already forgotten about Andy Bill completely. It seemed ages ago that their decrepit little house had been demolished and replaced by the Johnsons two-story one. The Johnsons had arrived and were friendly, clean and honest. They had three good-looking kids. Back then everyone had said good riddance to Andy Bill, his little brother Mark, their slovenly mother and their vicious dog, and had never thought about them again.

The events came back to me for the second time while I was translating one of Elias Papadimitrakopoulos's stories, "The Spanish Guitar." A poem published on the society page of the local newspaper reminds the narrator of Yiannis, a poor, thievish lad who like Andy Bill had died in the atrophied flower of his youth. Papadimitrakopoulos suggests that Yiannis and his family were Communists in those witch-hunting days around the time of the German Occupation and the Greek Civil War and, coincidentally, Andy Bill was called "The Socialist of the Neighborhood" by our parents, an appellation he had earned through his habit of expropriating a given child of a toy (such as Peter Meert of his hula hoop or my sister Ann of her red wagon), of removing it to a third child's lawn, of playing with it there and then of leaving it in that third child's hands. Wealth was continually being redistributed and parents had to be called in constantly to restore the *ancien régime* based on private property.

A standing dare in the neighborhood was to knock on Andy Bill's front door. No one, however, was required to wait on the doorstep until the door was opened. Not even Jimmy Cellini would have taken that one up. Still the intrepid had to contend with the shrieking curses of Andy Bill's mother—of his "old lady," to use his term—and especially with their terrier, which would be unleashed on the spot. It was reputed to be rabid.

Theirs was the only unvisited house on May Day and Halloween. On many of those Halloweens, around ten o'clock when the little kids were back inside, Dave and I would plaster their front door with mudballs. Then towards midnight Andy Bill and his brother would come out and smash every single last jack-o'-lantern on the block. The brave fathers watching *The Johnny Carson Show* would turn up the volume on their sets when they began to hear the *pop* of our hollow, lovingly carved crania being hurled down against the cement driveways.

Andy Bill had a bad case of acne well before the rest of us, already at the age of seven or eight. He may have had mixed blood (no one had ever seen his father), for his skin was darker than ours; but this was usually attributed to his uncleanliness. New older boys in the neighborhood would single him out the very first day for a pounding; new younger ones would, instinctively, keep their distance. Like a tyrant, he was hated and feared by all; unlike one, he lacked a well-trained house guard of stool-pigeons, henchmen and sycophants. Many hated Andy Bill because he was fatherless.

He wore the same flannel shirts and corduroys that we all did; only, his had unpatched torn elbows and grass-stained knees. Andy Bill's hands were grimy before playing. He cracked his knuckles constantly.

Little Mark was hated as much as Andy Bill was. The two brothers were inseparable. On those rare occasions when lacking players we grudgingly permitted Andy Bill to join our pick-up baseball games, he never consented to play unless Mark could as well. But Mark was too small. No compromises were ever made and someone would play catcher for both sides.

Then came the day when inspired by the celebrations of the Civil War Centennial we plotted a war, the North against the South. It was a sign of distinction to be for the South and Andy Bill's house was located at the far north end of 48th Street. No additional affront to our Confederacy was required and war was declared.

When we emerged from Jeannie Soyer's backyard, Andy Bill was waiting on his doorstep with a handful of gravel. The door opened and little Mark also appeared. Like his brother, Mark went over and scooped up a handful of gravel from the driveway. Each of us knew that mixed in with the gravel were pebbles, even rocks.

We approached them cautiously from the south with our sacks of mudballs. Our strategy, barked out in orders by Peter, was to bombard Andy Bill and Mark so severely that in raising their forearms to protect themselves they would be unable to attack us. We would charge our way up to them, turning the battle into a fistfight whose outcome would be certain.

The great battle had barely begun when it ended. Andy Bill and Mark threw their first fistfuls of gravel in our direction.... I screamed with pain, for just as I was sounding the Rebel war whoop through an aluminum-foil roller, a pebble struck my ear and lodged deeply within. Andy Bill and Mark streaked into their house. My friends gathered around trying to find the wound. I was holding my head and crying hysterically.

It didn't take my mother long to race out to the battlefield. Off she dragged me stumbling and sobbing across the lawn to our '57 Oldsmobile. We sped to Dr. Hill's office.

A pair of tweezers in the old doctor's steady hand dislodged the pebble. With his otoscope he peered in and around to verify that no damage had been done to the eardrum. But to this day I do not know whether the fact that I am slightly hard of hearing in my right ear—I was always called back twice by those ladies who went around the schools giving hearing tests—is a result of my Civil War injury.

What would have happened if I had been permanently deafened by the pebble? What would have happened if the pebble had been the tiniest bit smaller or bigger? These are conjectures that always fascinate me, how History might have been led onto utterly different paths had Chance but added or subtracted a thousandth of an inch.

And what would have happened if I had told the truth? For when we arrived home from the doctor's office I was set down in a chair and made to recount my version of the story. With tears welling in my eyes I told my mother how we had been playing tag when Andy Bill had thrown his stones.

And she believed me!

During my childhood years I often suffered from the friends who came into my life only to say good-bye and leave. No sooner were they settled into the school routine, halfway through the year, a lockermate assigned, their names written in on the typed enrollment sheet, than off they were swept, their fathers now transferred to Denver or to Omaha. Jon Kirkland was like that. One November morning Miss Noble introduced him to us. He was a wiry little boy with a bristly black crewcut. His jacket was strange, shiny, there was a jujitsu emblem embroidered on the back. Jon and I would walk home together, throwing snowballs at buses and girls; when school resumed after Christmas vacation his desk was empty. And there was Glenn Smith, a husky boy who wore glasses and plaid shirts. He had been in our class for about a year when his father had the heart attack. Miss Hamilton told us what to say, but Glenn never came back to school. In front of his house a real-estate sign appeared; the house was for sale, sold; no one knew where Mrs. Smith and Glenn had gone; no one ever received a letter.

And then there was Mary. She came into our fourth-grade class one winter day and had a family name that immediately all the boys ridiculed, cracking dirty jokes and making puns. She was short, stocky and dark-haired. Her skin was tanned deep copper in color and her eyes shone black like jewels of obsidian. What rent my heart, and made me dream of protecting her, was her timidity. I remember that afternoon when she had

to stand on stage at the school assembly. The principal handed her the prize; she looked out at us, then
down at the prize and her eyes remained there. A teacher
had to go up and lead her off. Many of the boys were
snickering behind their hands, for Mary was supposed
to make a speech.

I was as much in love with Mary as I could have
been at that age, which meant that no one else knew
and that I would observe her out of the corner of my
eye in class. Sometimes I caught her smiling to herself, and at those moments I would feel the urge to
spring out of my seat and run over and sit down next
to her, to share a private world from which everyone
else was excluded. In that world Mary told me secrets
and I caressed her hair and said:

"No one will ever know."

One evening that next summer I came across Mary
talking to Nancy near the privet hedge through which
we crawled when passing from 48th Street to 48th Street
Place.

When Nancy saw me, she announced that Mary was
moving out of town.

"What?"

"My dad's got a new job in Salt Lake City."

She talked to Nancy about the trip: Yellowstone Park,
the grandparents in Cheyenne, the station wagon was
already packed. What would school in Utah be like?
Mary's chubby hands were inanimate. Her seersucker
shorts were rumpled and grass-stained. There was a
little mist in her eyes: she and Nancy had become best
friends.

I didn't know what to say. I felt awkward and empty.
I looked down at my feet: the grass was uncut, the
ground spongy and damp.

How to say good-bye to her? All my life I have been plagued by an inability to put into my words of farewell all the emotion I have felt for a person. So often I have just turned and crawled back home through the hedge, with all my love and sorrow bottled up inside me.

When Françoise and I were exploring the back roads around Winterset for covered bridges and came across one upon which two frogs had been nailed, I immediately thought of Ted Jensen. Ted was the boy who first told me of the occult connection between frogs and warts, and of how a bad case could be cured. He himself had a horde on the back of his right hand—a dozen, perhaps two dozen brownish nodules which, along with his stutter and cropped hair, made Ted the butt of our jokes and the class untouchable. Boys shuddered theatrically when picking up from the blackboard tray the stub of chalk which Ted had just set down. Out on the playground, in the hand-holding circle games we formed, teachers forced us to make a place for him. No one, not even Goodwin, so heedless of the real world, dared to share a locker with him. Every new school year Ted had to sit ashamed and humiliated until the teacher assigned him to someone, inevitably to a new boy or to another outcast, rejected on grounds of body odor or bulk.

Had it not been for his warts and his stutter, however, Ted might have aspired to modest popularity, at least to acceptance. He had round brown eyes. His temperament was such that he never pushed or cut in line at the drinking fountain. When choosing up sides, we forgot his warts because he was a sure infielder. He could bring a ball upcourt. And Ted lived in an enchanted neighborhood: an overgrown ravine bordered his parents' backyard; there was a treehouse perched in an elm down there, underbrush to explore, even an abandoned sewer conduit into which one could dare, or dare someone else, to crawl.

It was down in that ravine that Ted, sneaking out of the house at night, performed his rites to cure himself of the warts. One rite involved catching a frog with his left hand, then rubbing it over the warts on his right hand while chanting:

"Cure thee warts, Frog! Cure thee warts, Frog! Cure thee warts, Frog!"

The rite had to be repeated on three successive nights.

"Th...th...th...th...that's why th...th...they're still th...th...th...there," Ted would explain, pointing with a dirty, unclipped fingernail at his mushroom patch of warts. He had gotten as far as two nights in a row several times, but, as he added, "ts...ts...ts...tsometimes you ju...ju...just can't catch a frog."

Back then my best friend was Paul Hofbauer, the son of a missionary for the First Federated Church. He lived two streets away from Ted's. One Friday night, when I was sleeping over at Paul's, we snuck out through his bedroom window and went down into the ravine. From there, crouching in the bushes, we imitated wild birds and animals, hoping to get the attention of Rita Gerstenmeyer, one of the girls in our class and Ted's next-door neighbor. Rita appeared not even at her window, but Ted was out of his house and down in the ravine in no time. With scarcely a word of greeting and despite his stutter he was soon outdoing us in both zeal and realism. The joke no longer seemed funny, so Paul interrupted Ted and asked him to show us how he caught his frogs.

Ted gave us an uneasy look.

"Come on, Ted," insisted Paul, "or I'll beat the living shit out of you."

I remember Ted, squatting, his hands jittering, trying to catch a frog. There were frogs all over the ravine that night. Ted, stiffly, timorously, made feeble stabs at them; off the frogs would spring; another would croak to his left or right; up Ted would leap, down Paul would order him. It was no use. Ted was afraid of frogs. Paul pushed him over on his back, gave him a kick, called him names, then we went home.

I had not stopped Paul and in addition, when I woke up the next morning, I realized that Ted had been lying to us all the time about catching frogs and curing warts. Everything had been made up: the midnight rites, the incantations. Ted had only wanted to be accepted.

"So did you apologize to him?" asked Françoise.

"Oh no. No, I didn't. Life just went on."

And as we were driving over the dusty gravel road back towards Winterset I recalled how in homeroom the next Monday morning Paul had told everyone about Ted and his fear of frogs.

Even after Steve Boyce and I were caught going through his sister's dresser in search of sanitary napkins, my father and mother never mustered the courage to come out straight with the facts about how babies are made. But little matter. I had already learned everything which at eleven must be learned, even much more than is strictly relevant to the labors of love and procreation.

I was schooled in "The Doctors' Club" founded by Dan Cooney, Jon Skidmore and Steve Schmitz at the Byron Rice Elementary School in March, 1964, and of which I became the fourth member shortly before its dissolution, due to summer vacation, in June of that same year. My brief membership permitted me to master the arcana of our club, a long list of dirty medical terms and the secret code we employed to transmit them to each other across the classroom.

The code, devised by Cooney, could be used as a written alphabet or as a sign language. It was never cracked, not even when our gym teacher, a rotund, balding, middle-aged bachelor who encouraged us to call him by his first name, Arnie, confiscated one of Skidmore's pornographic circulars, coded explanations given to him by one of his neighbors, a hoodlum who went to Tech High School. Usually Skidmore's circulars were impeccably clear, and to them I owe my first rudiments of sexual knowledge, but once he misconstrued the hoodlum's teachings and to this day a nauseating image haunts me. In one of those circulars, wrote Skidmore,

"If a man's penis is too short, then before copulation he inserts a thin metal straw into it so that the sperm will be able to reach its destination."

We knew such words because every Saturday morning Cooney, Skidmore, Schmitz and I met downtown at the Des Moines Public Library, where in the middle of the Reference Room, lying open on a wooden reading stand, was *Webster's Third International Dictionary.* Cooney and Schmitz brought the list of words to look up, Cooney culling his off the illustrations in *Gray's Anatomy,* a copy of which he had received for Christmas, and Schmitz having discovered where his parents hid their *Marriage Manual.* After a few Saturdays we had progressed from "testicle," "vagina" and "ovary" to the most esoteric medical terminology. Members of The Doctors' Club knew what "seminal vesicles" and "Fallopian tubes" were. A few Saturdays later we giggled over "lactiferous tubules" and "atretic follicles." Anything and everything having to do with the male and female genitalia—a category which, for us, comprised the mammae—was declared a dirty word, and I remember a despondent Cooney appearing one Saturday morning with the announcement that all he had managed to come up with were a few Latin terms for the veins and arteries of the penis. Still the words found their way onto our list.

All the erotic engravings in *Gray's*—of bladders, of testes, of rectums and so forth—were traced by Cooney onto onionskin paper. We stored the sheets in a manilla envelope stashed in Skidmore's locker. In that envelope as well was the much sought-after key to The Doctors' Club code. What Annie Peterson would have given to get her hands on it!

I still marvel today that she figured out the note she intercepted was about her. I had written it, in code, to Cooney, folded it twice, printed his name on the outside. Off it went across the classroom, passing from accomplice to accomplice, detouring around teacher's pets, while Mrs. Lawrence droned on about the natural resources of South America. Like all young teachers, Mrs. Lawrence kept her back turned to us too often—writing words on the blackboard, searching for capitals on the wall maps—whence the rapid progress of the note through the first ten hands. There were only five more to go when...Annie unfolded the note to read it!

She must have had an inkling of its contents. Did she then recognize the two "n"'s of her name, our code being alphabetic? A few classes later a similarly passed note arrived at my desk:

"Dear Johnny," she wrote. "I know your note was all about me so why don't you tell me what it says? I'm yours till Niagara Falls drinks Canada Dry! Luv, Annie."

It was just as well that Cooney never received the note. He would have passed it on to Skidmore and Schmitz, who would have made me the laughingstock of the playground. Some sentiments are best kept to oneself; decidedly I had gotten carried away. For how could The Doctors' Club have understood my attempt to describe, with the most beautiful words I knew, Annie Peterson's adorable little face and hands and breasts?

As I was reading the note that Denise had slipped into my desk, I felt my eyes squinting. She had written it on behalf of her best friend, Debbie Wolinski, with whom for the last two months I had been going steady, a relationship established officially and in due form by the gift of my identity chain. It was one of those liaisons in which for the first time a boy begins to scrutinize his sweetheart from the matrimonial perspective, even imagining her as the mother of his children. Debbie was short, soft, unathletic, but not too plump. She had long blond hair. Her voice was shrill and took some time to get used to; in addition she adored George Harrison, several pictures of whom she had cut out of magazines and pasted on her folders.

Denise's note stated that Debbie wanted me to kiss her, that afternoon after school, behind her house. The time designated puzzled me. Debbie knew that I had an appointment at the orthodontist's and that my mother would be picking me up from school. So in a note sent back through Denise, I reminded her of the appointment and promised to walk her home from school the next day. I signed my name and then added:

"P.S. I will."

That evening I spent alone in my bedroom mustering my courage. Kissing Debbie was a task towards which I felt both desire and revulsion, fear and duty. There were precedents: Denise herself had only one week back been kissed on the lips by Ned, and another of their friends, Carol Scarole, had made out several times with Steve Leeman down in her basement, the access to which her father precociously accorded her.

By nighttime I was simply lying there on the bed, my head propped up by two pillows. Then I took one of them and began practicing. The thought had just occurred to me. I nestled it in the crotch of my arm, squeezing the far side as if it were Debbie's shoulder. It was a foam-rubber pillow. From time to time I bent over and gave the cool, damp pillowcase a gentle peck. I mastered that type of kiss, then went on to the kiss on the lips.

The next day, all the way home, Debbie and I, holding hands, remained silent. When we arrived at the foot of her driveway, instead of parting as usual, we slowly walked up it, towards the back of the house. It was a terrifyingly beautiful spring day. Their lawn had been freshly mowed; three or four crab-apple trees were in bloom; both cars were missing from the double garage. I was sweating under my blast jacket, which I took off and draped over our books, under my arm.

When we reached the back part of the house, I put my arm around Debbie's shoulders. She cuddled up to me, resting her cheek against my sweater. Her hair, in the sunlight, was blinding white. She bore the strong scents of a perfume for teenagers, lavishly applied.

Without hesitating a moment more, I bent my head down and kissed her, and then held her there against me, clumsily with just one arm hugging her, struggling to maintain a grip on those heavy textbooks.

She was wearing raspberry lipstick.

That was all there was to it. There was no second kiss. We remained there for a few more minutes, then

I took my arm away. I had to be home by three-thirty so my mother wouldn't suspect anything.

Over the next few weeks we walked up the driveway nearly every afternoon. Then one day Debbie said good-bye. I got my identity chain back through Denise.

I saw Debbie fifteen years later.

"We have new neighbors now!" announced my mother as we were coming back from the airport. "Hardly of a better sort than the last ones. The Wolinskis, do you remember them? You used to go to school with their kids."

I couldn't believe my ears.

"Mrs. Wolinski is a Shapiro, the family that has all those stationery stores. It's one of the oldest families in Des Moines. Can you believe that Mr. Wolinski tried to embezzle his father-in-law's company?! In order to get their money back from the insurance companies, the Shapiros...."

The next day, opening the front door to pick up the evening newspaper, I caught sight of Debbie, surrounded by three toddlers, out in the Wolinskis' front yard. She was wearing a garishly colored smock and was pregnant again. Her hair was as long and blond as ever.

She began heading indoors with the children, her back to me, so I called out to her.

We met over the row of privet dividing the two lawns. She asked me how I was doing, I replied, then I asked her. But before we could say much more, the eldest child began tugging at her thigh, beating it, whining, dragging her away. We hurriedly said good-bye and although nothing was definitely set I imagined we would meet again to talk over old times. But not once over the next month did I see her car in her parents' driveway.

That I never managed to hold Karen's hand during any of the Cinema Club movies that spring was not entirely due to my ineptitude in amorous matters. First, there was Miss Brown, gripping her flashlight, walking the aisles in search of couples holding hands or boys who had managed to slip an arm around their girlfriend's shoulders. Off to the vice principal's office the young man would go, from which he would emerge an hour later with at least a letter for his parents to sign and sometimes with a three-day suspension from school.

Then there was Karen herself. She felt that "going all the way" (as she termed the act of holding hands) would irreparably endamage our friendship, that our long, intimate talks, as we walked home from school, would end.

"Please! Don't!" she would plead, repulsing another of my ruses—dangling my hand alongside hers and letting the ups and downs of our strides swing them into contact. "Let's just be friends!"

How I wanted to show Karen that holding hands or even kissing could only strengthen the foundations of our mutual affection, that human caress was like a commitment, that Janet Sunden had been kissed and was still going steady with Ted Kepler, that another of her friends, Brenda Saintsbury, had decided to be kissed and was only waiting for the propitious moment, next

Friday she hoped, when her mother would be out playing bridge.... The tension gripping every muscle in my body upon the mere sight of Karen, across the room in biology class, in the stands at a baseball game (where I would be pitching or playing first base), and especially as she ran up to me in the morning before homeroom, her hair in a pixie and wearing culottes, was becoming unbearable.

Rob had the same problem with Diana. Often we compared stratagems and setbacks, whispering to each other after gym class in the locker room.

"We were trying to cross Hickman Road," reported Rob, "there was a lot of traffic...I grabbed her hand and started leading her across...I wasn't thinking about getting a piece...but Di screamed, the cars screeched to a halt...out of one of them jumped this guy...so last night on the phone she said she wanted to break up...okay we broke up...then this morning she said everything was okay. Do you think that's what she really means? Maybe she's giving me the green light?"

She wasn't.

So Rob and I settled down. We were going steady, after all, with girls our mothers had no doubts about. We started dressing up in sta-press pants and doing our homework. I began writing poems to Karen, three or four a day, slipping them, when she wasn't looking, into one of her folders.

Then one day Rob suggested we make a bet:

"A dollar I can make out with Di down in her basement before you can with Karen down in hers."

"But I've never even held her hand."

"Both of them want us to. Di told me so."

I never would have gone through with it had Karen

herself not urged me on.

"Let's go down to the recreation room and listen to records," she said as we were walking up the driveway.

I had never been inside her house. Up to then we had always sat out on her front steps.

Down in the basement she put on something by The Animals. She adjusted the volume until the song was barely audible, as if to create a mood. I strained to catch the lyrics, hoping to find a clue, a confirmation of Karen's intentions. Staring straight ahead, her hands folded in her lap, she sat there on the couch.

I asked: "Will your mother be coming home soon?"

"Not until five," she answered.

At that I draped my arm around her, pulled her over and kissed her on the lips. Though Karen kept her lips pursed, always a bad sign, I did close my eyes and gracefully weave my head about, like a snake. My face was flushing with passion and I like to think my bud of a penis was in erection.

When I had withdrawn an inch from her lips and was preparing for a second kiss, she struggled out of my embrace and snapped:

"Look at your watch."

I pretended not to understand.

"It's three-thirty. Did you win your bet?"

Karen's sobs drowned out The Animals.

It took us three weeks to break up and Karen instigated it. I was late in meeting her after English class; she claimed I didn't care for her anymore.

I didn't see Karen for three years after that: we had gone to different high schools. As I entered the waiting room of the dermatologist's office, I saw Karen rising to follow the nurse. We greeted each other hurriedly. Karen glanced back at me as she was rounding the corner. For the next twenty minutes, a *Golf Digest* in my lap, I sat there wondering whether she would be finished before I was called in. Then my turn came, but after Dr. Thompson had squeezed my pimples and I was leaving, I peeked into the waiting room, hoping that Karen would still be there. And she was not.

Though she occasionally mentioned it, I no longer remember the name of the cursive writing method by which my mother learned her penmanship. Of it she retained till the end of her life every sweep, every sharp loop, every crossbar. When she signed her name to a check or to a Christmas card, every new letter was traced equidistant to the last; there was no letting the "r" run; the middle initial particularly impressed me, an "E" penned like a "3" backwards and at a slant.

The last time I admired my mother's penmanship was when I noticed a slate on the kitchen wall. It was one of those imitation antiques, a turn-of-the-century grammar-school writing slate, the size of a piece of paper, bordered with strips of walnut. Dangling on a blue string from a hole at the top there was a slender piece of gray chalk, sharpened by use to a point and with a luster on its surface. My mother had bought the slate at that antique shop in West Des Moines, owned by one of her friends, where to pass the time she sometimes worked in the afternoon.

On the slate my mother had written a message of encouragement to herself, a short poem with rhymes. Tears came to my eyes when I read the words; they were the last words she would write. For three weeks I avoided looking at the slate. Then, at the kitchen door, leaving for the airport, I set my bags down, walked back, and removed the slate from the wall.

"Let's leave it the way it is," said Françoise when she saw it.

I have just checked and we have already bought, long ago, most of the things still listed on the slate, which hangs in our kitchen, near the sink, on a panel which hides pipes and the water meter. The piece of chalk is now a stub; dust sits on the thin upper edge of the walnut frame; the slate hangs slightly crooked.

Now and then I feel guilty about having wiped away my mother's last written words. Did she know one of us would read them? Did she expect the slate to be kept that way in memory of her? As usual, the letters had been traced out so beautifully.

Except for those few words, I never learned what my mother thought about death. That final year she only signed her name to the postcards my father wrote; some of the examinations were humiliating; she was afraid of having to vomit in public; friends organized a prayer group and a laying on of hands. One day during Christmas vacation my mother said:

"If something happens to me, don't come back home."

I didn't know how to answer her. I sat there fingering the handle of my coffee mug, staring at it. Words of encouragement were in my mind, but I couldn't bring myself to use them.

"Aluminum" was a word my mother couldn't have pronounced correctly had her life depended on it. The word "linoleum" she massacred. Whenever the words came up in an afternoon chat my mother asked for more coffee, or fumbled in her purse for cigarettes, or pleaded her inability to get past the second syllables with a laugh and a look imploring one of the ladies to say it for her.

"Jan, li-no-le-um!" would demonstrate Mrs. Tanner from across the room, always eager to get one up on someone, anyone.

My mother would play at pronouncing it, tell them about her father not letting her sit down for supper until she had gotten several words with "r"'s and "l"'s in them right, and all the time feel like running out of the room and sobbing herself to sleep in her bedroom back home, way back home, in Lewiston, Idaho. My mother hated the words "aluminum" and "linoleum" as much as she did chicken livers and eggplant.

The chicken livers had something to do with sorority hazing.

The eggplant went back to one spring evening in 1943 when my mother came home late from high school, just in time for supper. My grandfather had taken his seat at the head of the long walnut table, tucked his napkin under his collar and picked up his fork. My grandmother was setting everything out: a large bowl of jello, a pot of spaghetti, and a mashed vegetable that my mother had never seen before.

"What's this stuff?" she asked, sniffing her nose at it while serving herself some jello.

"Eggplant!" replied my grandmother. "I'm just delighted. Ernie was able to bring some back from Seattle. But I had to give him a shoe coupon for it."

"Take some and pass it," ordered my grandfather.

My mother poked at the goo (my grandmother always overcooked vegetables), then took a bite off the tip of her spoon.

"Yuk!" she cried and then, as she had been shown how to do, placed her napkin against her lips as if to wipe them gently—and spit the eggplant back out.

My grandfather got up, picked up the serving dish full of stewed eggplant and walked around to her side of the table.

"Eat the eggplant!" he commanded.

He wrested the napkin from her, unwadded it, seized her spoon, scooped up the half-salivated mush and threatened to force-feed it to her. My mother beat his hand away.

"So that's how it is!" he shouted. "I'll teach you to eat this damned eggplant!"

With that, he grabbed a fistful of the steaming food, pried my mother's jaws open with his other hand and began stuffing the eggplant into her mouth, ceasing only when she had started gagging, coughing, vomiting the eggplant over the table.

That is how I imagine a story which my mother would tell in a very different tone, indeed one of exuberance. She could laugh off that memory, as she could her stuttering pronunciations of "linoleum" and "aluminum," as she could the novels she read (despite her English major), as she could her patriotism and Republican vote.

And such were just a few of the things that we kidded

her about, unmercifully. Who imagines before it is too late the destruction waged by trespassers (even innocent ones) over those secret pathways into another's world?

I was the last trespasser, just one day before she died. Ann, Joan, my father and my grandmother were still on their way to the hospital; I was sitting alongside my mother's bed, a menu in my hand, trying to cheer her up by joking about the French names the hospital kitchen had given to some of the dishes.

"Here's one you won't like," I exclaimed. "Thank goodness they've got what they call 'carrots à la cream.' They're offering a *gratin d'aubergines*."

"What's that?" asked my mother, indifferently.

She gazed over at me for the first time in a while.

"*Eh bien,* a *gratin d'aubergines* is an eggplant casserole!"

My mother's mouth formed the word "yuk" and she smiled feebly. Then she sighed, her eyes rolling back, out of sight, her eyelids slowly descending. Only then did the thought occur to me of how much laughter had to do, if with the avoidance of certain truths, with my mother's will to live and with her dignity.

The heroic version, which subsisted in the minds of some even two weeks after it had been formally refuted by the Rev. Robert Kramer at the funeral, was that Smitty had fallen on the football field, a few yards short of the end zone, the touchdown pass bobbling to a stop. When he failed to rise, the players gathered round, the coaches came running; someone sprinted all the way up to the school to call an ambulance; but it was too late, Smitty had lost consciousness, Smitty was in agony, Smitty was dead.

What actually happened was that after the third football practice of the day (those notorious summer practices, three times a day, in the suffocating heat) Smitty had gone home, called his sweetheart Debbie and canceled their date, then lay down on his bed, his cool, neatly-made bed in that dark, air-conditioned room, and never arose. When his parents came home from golf they found the untouched sandwich on the counter, his cutoff jeans and T-shirt strewn before his door, the lights on everywhere.

Smitty was dead. He was the first one of us to go. The church was packed. There were several eulogies. Somewhere in the midst of the mourners sat the football coach. It had been hot, the people said, too hot. Everywhere in Iowa that summer the corn had withered.

Smitty is dead. He was the first one of us to go. The

sole image I have retained of him goes back to a summer in which he must have been ten or eleven. He
was standing at home plate, aiming his bat at a ball
poised on a peculiar sort of stand, a thin, waist-high,
hard-rubber spike with an aluminum tip driven into
the ground. His father, a little way off, was observing
and correcting him. Some little kid out towards the
fences was fielding Smitty's hits.

I remember how his father would, from time to time,
go over to the other side of the plate and put his arms
around his son's, as if they were to bat the same ball
together. He was showing his son how to cock his bat,
how to bring it around smoothly and levelly, without
flinching, without tucking his left elbow in, striding
firmly forward with his left foot, his wrists quick, snapping,
his eye clear. Smitty was one of the better batters in
our Little League. Short and stocky, he played catcher
for the Yankees.

But he had been in a slump. For three games he had
gone hitless, swinging at wild pitches or not swinging
at all. He had been stepping out, his left foot drifting
off to the left side of the batter's box as the pitcher
was winding up, then jerking even further as the ball
came speeding towards the catcher's mitt. Stepping out
was always a sign of fear, the fear of being hit by a
fastball.

It is one of the worst fears a boy can have.

I also knew that fear. Three or four times I conquered
it, four or five times it returned.

So when I am obliged to think of death I often see
Smitty standing there at home plate, aiming his bat at a
ball on a spike. At first the image of that odd accessory
makes me chuckle, but then I see that Smitty *actually is*

only standing there, his bat cocked, his knuckles white from gripping the handle, his jaw set, his eyes glassy. Not the slightest breeze ruffles his uniform. Not the slightest word of advice comes from his father. Everything is motionless and then everything disappears.

I would be leaving for good in a few days, so I mustered my courage and called Kathy. She was distant and formal on the phone, but said I could come. Objects and obligations still bound her to me: the books she had never returned, the loose, frayed ends of our story. It was our last chance, and she knew it, to tie up neat little bundles of pain and delusion and cast them into the sea.

I sat in an armchair and she stood across the room in a corner, her arms folded across her chest. Her features seemed sharp, angular; her skin tight and pale. She had lost even more weight. I wondered, without daring to ask, if she had attained that perfectly flat stomach she so desired—like a man's, without that layer of fat which all women, being childbearers, carry upon their abdomens.

I asked if she were still selling tickets. The last time I had seen her had been at the Community Playhouse. When I arrived at the window to pick up the reservations, she was the one who suddenly appeared to hand them to me. Over the phone, when I had ordered them, not a word of recognition had been pronounced. And yet it must have been her. I, in any case, suspecting nothing, had not paid any attention to the voice. Months and months had gone by. She had worked in two other places since then and was now selling skis in a sporting goods store.

"But in August we'll be leaving," she added.

Kathy left the room and returned with a pile of poetry books and, I had completely forgotten it, that expensive guide to New England. We had bought it together, in a bookstore in Cambridge, that week I had flown out to see her.

"I'll be moving here," I had said, "so let's go ahead and buy this one. It looks like the most detailed. There are pages and pages of history for every town."

Kathy set the books on a chair near the door.

"I hope you'll forgive me," she said, "but I have things to do."

It was the phrase that summed her up perfectly. She took a denim jacket off a hook and shouldered her purse. I expected her to take a quick look in the hall mirror, but then realized that in this apartment there was no hall mirror.

"Can we go now?" she insisted.

I only had one last thing to say and took the piece of paper from my pocket. I had written down a line from the first book that Kathy had given to me. I re-read the quotation, then folded the piece of paper in two. I got up. At the door I handed her the note and said:

"Read this, but only after I'm gone."

We walked down the flight of stairs, said good-bye at the bottom without shaking hands, then I got into my car and drove off.

It was drizzling and in the rearview mirror I saw her running across the road, clutching her arms across her chest. I braked to watch her, but then she disappeared behind a row of maple trees.

The quotation was: "It was no ordinary joy, it was a sublime, absurd and unjustifiable gladness."

II. THE VIEW FROM THE UPPER WINDOW

Joan thought it was Mr. Kent who had died, I thought it was Mrs. Rabie.

"I'm almost sure it was Mr. Kent," she insisted.

"But he wasn't that old. He was still teaching high school. Mrs. Rabie was in her seventies."

"I know. But I'm positive it was Mr. Kent."

A silence fell, we cut into our pizzas.

Hadn't someone moved in across the street, just before we left the old neighborhood?

"It must have been into Mrs. Rabie's house. Why would Mrs. Kent have moved away?"

"To find something smaller," replied Joan.

We gave up. Eighteen years had passed. I poured us each a glass of Chianti.

Joan could not remember everyone in my stories.

"But I remember Nancy's mother really well. What amazes me now, when I think of it, is that I used to sit in her house all day long watching television. Didn't she ever get tired of me?"

Mr. Matthews had bought a reclining armchair for their living room. We took turns playing on it, pushing and pulling the levers, popping up the footrest, turning the chair into a bed.

"Why haven't you ever written about the Hanscombs?"

We went directly to the heart of the matter: the unforgettable family letters they sent at Christmas, Mrs. Hanscomb breast-feeding baby Glenn out on the front porch, the mystery about the broken garage door, Mr. Hanscomb embezzling the church he worked at, his collection of dirty magazines down in the basement.

"He started showing me one," laughed Joan, "I screamed, ran up the stairs, tore across Ruth and Ernie's lawn, found Dad upstairs putting on the screen windows. 'Dad!' I shouted, 'do you know what Mr. Hanscomb has got in his basement?' He said he'd take care of it."

"Did he?"

"I don't really know," replied Joan.

We moved on to the subject of our junior-high and high-school romances, the fact that our mother had never accepted any of our girlfriends and boyfriends.

"Remember how she would pretend to be sick and not even come down to say hello?"

"I don't think she was pretending," replied Joan.

The worst incident occurred one Saturday morning when Donni came over to help us move into the new house. My hopes of showing my mother how nice Donni was shattered over the question whether protective plastified paper should be tacked, scotch-taped or simply placed in a kitchen drawer.

"What ever happened to her?" asked Joan.

"I have no idea."

The three of us had each moved away after high school, Joan to Dallas, Ann to Nashville, I to several places, then to Paris. The years had gone by; we were now at that age when the first major period of our lives seemed detached from the continuum of time: for seventeen years we had lived in one place, Des Moines. Des Moines was the city of our childhood and adolescence.

"But you seem more attached to Des Moines than I do," remarked Joan. "Actually, if Dad didn't live there,

I'd never go."

The waiter, standing alongside our table, his head cocked to the side, an ironic smile on his face, overtly eavesdropping on our English conversation, handed us each a menu so that we could select our desserts. I chose a *zuppa inglese*, Joan a chocolate mousse.

"Coffee afterwards?" he asked.

I looked at Joan, she nodded.

"Deux cafés!" I ordered, turning away.

"Perhaps because I've lived abroad so long. Still, if I were to live in the United States again, I can't really see myself anywhere else."

The remark provoked a sudden sadness in Joan.

She looked at me inquisitively; in a moment she asked:

"Would you like to be buried there?"

I thought I knew the answer to that question, but for some reason I fell silent—perhaps because it was my little sister who had asked me—, then finally replied:

"I don't know."

The waiter brought our desserts.

Miss Hamilton asked someone else to read the paragraph, the same paragraph, again. I whispered to Rex, looked behind him out the window to our left. Black branches of the elm; through the black branches the sky, gray, shiny, harsh to the eyes. Then I noticed the panes of glass, the drops of rain which had spattered there, dried, leaving crescents of grime and dust. The pale green muntins, one rising, one crossing. Then I looked back at Miss Hamilton.

She was looking at me so I smiled and she said:

"Are there any of you who would like to read something else?"

My hand shot up, Rex glanced at me, at Miss Hamilton, back at me, slowly his hand rose....

Miss Hamilton stood up, waddled towards me, the others scooting their chairs aside so she could pass. She was an enormous woman, her body two balloons (as we said), no cheeks, several chins, her eyes black like a snowman's, her hair cropped short like a boy's. She was wearing a flowered dress, faded, yards and yards of washed-out cloth. She hovered over me. I smiled again; she told me to get up and to come with her to the back of the room.

At the back of the room was a large walk-in closet, a storeroom in which books and supplies were stacked. Miss Hamilton opened the door to the closet, told me to stand still for a moment, waddled off, came back with a chair, guided me inside with the nails of her fingers. She set me down on the chair and she said:

"If you would really like to read something else, sit here for a moment."

I thanked her eagerly, but was given a strangely glaring look. Then Miss Hamilton turned off the light and closed the door.

I immediately stood up, started feeling in the darkness for the door, for the light. I was sure she had turned off the light by accident, I kept groping for the door, then remembered her glaring look, groped my way back to the chair: I was being punished.

Or was I?

I stood up again, remained standing almost shivering, tears coming against my will to my eyes. What if the door suddenly opened and the others found me crying? I remained standing, fighting back the tears, one hand poised for reassurance on a shelf along the wall, the other on the back of the chair. Only after some time did I notice the thin crack of light under the door, come to distinguish the shapes of objects around me. Through the door, through the wall, came the distant sound of one of my classmates reading. She will be back in a minute, I started thinking, the light was an accident, she will be back in a minute with something for me to read, back as soon as the others have finished. I sat back down, trying to breathe calmly, folded my hands in my lap, watched the door.

If I am not being punished, I thought, then I can turn the light back on and maybe find something here to read. Maybe that's what I'm supposed to do.

I stood up, waited long like that, straining to hear what was going on in the classroom, waited long, long, finally sat back down in the darkness. I was being punished.

I sat for how long? At one point I heard chairs sliding, drawers opening, slamming, my classmates marching out of the classroom home. I stood up, waited, but Miss Hamilton didn't come. I was being punished, had to stay, had to stay after school. I sat back down, began crying.

I cried time away.

I cried till time came back.

Finally Miss Hamilton opened the door, asked me whether I had learned my lesson. I said I had, but refused to look at her. She sent me off to pick up my books and out the door.

The patrol boys and girls had long gone home; the traffic was piling up on Beaver Avenue. I pushed the stoplight button, waited. I knew the drivers would be angry; I pushed the button again. And again. And when the light had turned green and I had walked to the other side of the street I waited, then pushed the button again. Only then did I see my mother, whom apparently Miss Hamilton had called, watching me from our car parked a short distance away.

Mrs. Hilman, or "Widow Hilman" as we called her behind her back, let our club—the Des Moines Detectives—solve mysteries down in her basement, which contained countless stacks of old magazines and a fragrant cedar closet full of hats and winter garments. Nearly every afternoon she hired us, against a plate of freshly baked cookies, to find a certain pair of brown woolen gloves or a blue ribbon, and once even a photograph, buried in one of a couple hundred *Life* magazines, of Mamie and Ike motorcading down our own Locust Street. We knew well that rummaging through old clothes and magazines was hardly an activity worthy of our sleuthing skills, but what else could we do? It had been an exceptionally calm summer. Jimmy Cellini hadn't set fire to any garages in over a year; his sister Bernadette had stopped torturing dogs; and what about Peter Meert, the neighborhood thief, who upon joining our organization became a partisan of private property?

Such was the misery that had befallen us, such was the mean, servile detective work we were engaged in when one Saturday afternoon Mrs. Hilman came downstairs to ask if we had seen the handle to her outdoor water faucet.

Nobody had.

"Strange...," she said. "It was there this morning when I watered the lawn. I'll go back up and take another look."

After a while she came back downstairs and repeated her question.

Jeannie Soyer asked if she had looked in the garage. Peter thought it might have fallen into the flowers. My sister Ann wondered whether Mrs. Hilman had unknowingly put it in her apron pocket.

She hadn't.

From which Nancy Matthews, Vice President, deduced that it had been stolen.

Whereupon Goodwin Craig, Scientist of the Des Moines Detectives, awoke out of his logarithms to announce in his giggly voice that he would go up immediately and "lift" fingerprints.

It was our greatest investigation. Every day for two weeks we combed the neighborhood in search of the missing water faucet handle. We explored gardens and porches. We collected alibis and hypotheses. Goodwin lifted innumerable fingerprints. Peter cut through the brush with his Swiss Army knife.

A few neighbors such as Mrs. Boyce, the German professor's wife, accused the O'Connell sisters of having once again practiced their black arts. But eventually we reasoned that the two old maids could just as easily have burned up every single last lawn on the block if they had so desired, and surely without having to employ tactics so indirect as making water faucet handles disappear. In any case this was an unverifiable conjecture, for who would have dared to subpoena Helen and Ruth O'Connell?

Then, two weeks later to the day, while groping in the flowers under the faucet, I bolted up with the missing handle in my hand. There it had always been, though no one could believe it, lying hidden under the ageratums! How many times had it escaped our scrutiny? Not to forget that of Mrs. Hilman, who now, clasping and unclasping her hands, was nearly running to set up the sprinkler. But it was too late to save her parched lawn.

Thereafter, whenever we played over at Mrs. Hilman's house, I would notice that water faucet handle on the counter every time we walked through the kitchen on our way downstairs. I would try to hurry on by it, blushing, ashamed of myself, for it had taken me two whole weeks to figure out a way to return it without her and the others' knowing that it was I who had, for no real reason at all, removed it from the tap, put it in my pocket and taken it home.

I'll never forget those trips my father and I took to Chicago and to Kansas City, where for one or two nights we stayed at the same hotel as the New York Yankees. There we would be, Saturday morning, signing in at the registration desk, when Whitey Ford would come strolling through the lobby or Yogi Berra lumber up and ask the clerk for his key. I always had plenty of autograph paper in my pockets and thus was able to amass doubles, triples, even quadruples of all the great stars of those years. I used to give Bobby Richardsons away. Hector Lopez I had six or seven times over. Even the two angry young men of the Yankees back then, Roger Maris and Bob Cerf, who reputedly never signed autographs for anyone, each gave me his one Sunday morning when respectfully I approached and asked very politely.

All morning long, before the afternoon game, I hung around the lobby hunting for autographs. I learned not a few things about human nature. One year there was a shortstop just up from the minor leagues, who without my knowing it had been sitting in the lobby reading a newspaper. (He hadn't come out on baseball cards yet.) I was leaning on a pillar, my eyes on the elevators, when a voice behind me said:

"Hey there boy."

When I turned, a blond-haired man in a plaid sports coat motioned me nearer, then asked:

"You want my autograph?"

Keeping my distance, I handed him my piece of paper. The man signed his name slowly, neatly, at an angle.

When I got the piece of paper back and looked at the signature, I waved at the other boys to come over. It was Tom Thresh, the shortstop they had brought up to replace Tony Kubek: a ground ball, ricocheting off an infield pebble, had a few weeks before struck Kubek in the Adam's apple, nearly killing him.

The other boys were for the most part local kids, many from the poorest neighborhoods, who had managed to learn where the Yankees stayed when in town. If they behaved themselves, usually they were allowed by the bellboys to loiter in the lobby with the boys like me who were staying at the hotel. I was always embarrassed when one of those kids asked where I lived.

"In Des Moines."

"You mean you're staying in this hotel!" the boy would exclaim.

Sometimes one of us spotted a star trying to sneak down the far stairs and out the side door. After him we would go, in stiff strides just short of sprinting, dodging groups of chatting businessmen. In no time the bellboys would also arrive, free the cornered leftfielder and line us up against the wall.

"Are your parents staying here?" they would ask each one of us in turn.

Everyone would answer yes, but the bellboys, looking us over, would know who was staying at the hotel and who wasn't. The ejected ones would then station themselves on the sidewalks outside, before the entrances, where with a series of wild cries they would alert the others, posted around the corners, whenever a New York Yankee left the hotel. The commotion would be intense and long-lasting; passersby would be jostled, injured; often the player would be held up for at least a half hour before he managed, ever scribbling his name, to edge his way over and into a taxi and speed away.

Then came the trip to Kansas City when my father and I had breakfast with Casey Stengel. We were eating pancakes in the coffee shop when in walked the great manager, a bow-legged old man with a tanned, leathery face. Casey shook hands with several astonished youngsters, then arrived at our booth. I bolted up, a sheet of paper in my hand.

"Sit yourself down, son," he said, winking at my father. "You folks mind if I join you?"

It was mid-season and things looked pretty good. Whitey's arm had been a little sore, but his win-loss record was better than last year's. Mickey had come out of his slump. Tony was out for the rest of the season, but the new boy, Thresh, was already batting over .300. Yogi was Yogi. Had I seen the doubleheader on T.V. last week? Yes, Mr. Stengel. Well, that just went to show how an old team with fresh blood could work together. The day looked nice, there was some crosswind, but not too much, Whitey would be on the mound, he liked pitching in K.C. You fellows got good seats?

"Yes, we have," replied my father. "Along the first-base line."

Casey chuckled, tossled my hair with his calloused hand, waved a salute, went on. I watched him greeting people at the other tables; his gestures were broad, his eyes scintillated; in a short while he vanished around a corner.

Sometimes, when feeling discouraged, I imagine myself

as I did back then, a pitcher for the New York Yankees, a tingling in my flesh, Casey giving my arm a punch, the bases loaded, he's going to let me pitch it out.

"Give the son-of-a-bitch your fastball," he commands, then turns on his heel, strides back to the dugout.

I look over at Thresh; he gives me the thumbs-up sign. I step to the rubber. Yogi signals a curveball; I shake my head; between the bars of his catcher's mask he's grinning.

"Here's the creampuff!" he shouts in encouragement.

He adjusts his position.

Ted Kluszewski takes another half-swing.

Back then, I would no longer be afraid of Ted Kluszewski.

I don't think I was attracted to her because out of
envy she was hated by the rest of the class. She was
short, a little plump, but had beautiful eyes and two
long pigtails that came down nearly to the small of
her back. During the uproar which ensued whenever
Mrs. Lawrence left the classroom, Sally would continue
working on her exercises or open the book she had
checked out of the library or, her hands clasped in
front of her, just sit there observing us. In those moments I did the same, knowing my hopes were slim if
I too got out of hand. She seemed a year or two older
than the rest of us, though in fact she was a year younger.
She had moved to Des Moines in mid-year from Chicago; there were rumors, never confirmed, that she had
skipped a grade.

She immediately replaced Kathleen Landureau as the
teacher's pet. From that first week on Mrs. Lawrence
began reading Sally's compositions aloud, interrupt-
ing the narrative here and there with remarks about
well-turned phrases and apt transitions. The boys, especially, sat there grimly, heads cradled in their hands,
eyes staring straight ahead. I did not understand all
the words that Sally used, but I marveled at her de-
scriptions, so full of rare adjectives that while listen-
ing to them I daydreamt myself into a forest, a path-
less, paradisical forest.

Then came the clever ending, which Mrs. Lawrence
usually had to explain.

In short time the word got around that Sally was rich. At first we thought her father sold cars, then we learned he owned the dealership. It is true that Sally dressed for school as if it were Sunday school; she had a white mohair sweater which from across the classroom seemed so soft that in bed at night I lay my head upon it, in my imagination. Even during gym class she kept her necklace on, a golden chain with a peculiar, geometric ornament. At first the other girls flocked about her; she was invited to stay all night at their houses. Later Sally was always alone; on the playground the girls giggled without her, strode in groups out the door after school while Sally was still putting her books away. In time Theresa, the fat girl, became Sally's best and only friend.

They walked home together and sometimes I spied on them by keeping to the other side of Urbandale Avenue, a block behind. Sally's family had moved into a large house there, near 44th Street, and past that house I rode my bike whenever I could, even on errands for my mother which should have taken me the other way, up 48th Street to Mrs. Tanner's or over to Cody's, just two blocks away. Whenever we drove past in the car, out of the corner of my eye I scrutinized the windows; once Sally and her German shepherd were playing on their long, sloping lawn.

"That's the new girl in our class," I remarked to my mother, searching her face for approval.

Back then, as today, an incapability of asserting myself kept me from approaching Sally even through Theresa or by means of inquiring glances cast slyly at propitious moments. Our desks had been arranged along three walls of the classroom; Sally's desk faced mine directly. But our eyes never seemed to meet. Whenever Mrs. Lawrence forced the boys to pair up with the girls, I always drew someone else's name out of the hat. And when on the playground a mitten dropped out of Sally's pocket, though I knew it was hers I handed it over to Mrs. Lawrence for the Lost & Found.

"Now thank him," she said when Sally stood up to claim the mitten.

She thanked me, that was all.

One night, for our homework, we were to describe an everyday object in such a way that the others would have to guess what it was. I sat in my room thinking for a while. I thought I might like to write about a clock, the clock in the kitchen. But I couldn't get started, so finally I gave up, went into the kitchen, noticed immediately that the clock was not how I had imagined it, thought that perhaps I should start all over again, asked my mother anyway for help. The description which resulted, chosen the next day by Mrs. Lawrence as the best, was written nearly in its entirety by my mother.

An admirative silence fell when I had finished reading it aloud and, glancing at Mrs. Lawrence, I had the impression that she herself did not know what the object was.

"So what is it?" she asked twice, surveying my classmates' faces.

No one said a word. Dick, Chuck, Ian, Clate—all my friends were staring, stunned. Skidmore elbowed Schmitz, gestured towards me, whispered something. Then Sally's hand shot up like a bayonet.

"A clock!" she cried, even before Mrs. Lawrence could call on her.

And she was looking intensely, not at Mrs. Lawrence, but at me.

Sally and her family moved, a week or two later, to Seattle.

Ten years later, at home for Christmas vacation, I bought a stereo in a small shop in downtown Des Moines from a man who turned out to be Sally's uncle. I had noticed his name on the receipt, turned back, asked.

"The last time I heard," he reported, "Sally was going to school in Minneapolis."

"Do you have her address by chance?"

"We don't see that side of the family much."

It was an uncommon name, so I called Information and inquired. The girl took quite a while, then replied that under that name no numbers were listed in either Minneapolis or Saint Paul.

"Are you sure about the spelling?" she asked.

"Well, put a 's' in place of the first 'z.'"

"Still no numbers," she replied. "Sorry."

There was a note of sadness in her voice, as if she had imagined why I wanted the number.

"Maybe you'll figure out another way to contact the person," she added.

"Maybe," I replied, then thanked her and slowly set the receiver on the hook.

They lived on the other side of the Farnys, next door to Andy Bill. The husband, who must have been fifty years old, we only rarely saw. Perhaps he worked on a night shift or was frequently out of town. Whenever we rang their doorbell for Halloween or to sell tickets for the school or for Cub Scouts, it was always the wife who opened the door. She was short and moon-faced, with curls of reddish-brown hair crowning her forehead. Her skin seemed slick and shiny, pale, like porcelain; often she was wearing a nightgown or a housedress. She would stand just in front of the darkness, which was tinged with the distant blue glow of a television. Behind her, a buffet piled with dishes was barely visible. They had a black poodle which would appear, blinking and curious.

Seeing us dressed up as ghosts and buccaneers, the wife would stick out her hand to stop our tricks, then hand us each a piece of candy and close the door. The porch light would go off; slowly we would move away, looking at each other, sensing the frosty air on our cheeks and feeling uneasy and somehow punished. And yet every year we returned.

They had a daughter, away at school. I only remember her there one summer, always out on the front steps reading books. The family kept their lawn neatly trimmed, but it was a high-school boy from another neighborhood who brought his lawn mower over in a car. The same boy shoveled their driveway in the winter. None of us younger kids would have asked, anyway. There was something about the house that like a magnet drew us towards it; so strongly that most of the time, especially whenever alone, we kept our distance.

We knew their names, that was all. On muggy summer evenings when everyone was outside, the mothers and fathers on their front steps drinking ice-tea and beer, the children playing catch or hide-and-go-seek in the yards, sometimes the couple started down the driveway in their Studebaker.

"There they go," someone would utter, raising his eyebrows.

But the couple always turned down 48th Street, never up it. A silence would fall, then the chatting would liven. My mother would say:

"At least they could wave."

They never waved. They never spoke, as far as I know, to anyone. When the Cellinis moved out and the new neighbors, the Packards, invited everyone over for a backyard get-together, the woman returned the invitation by mail, having written in neat letters under the "R.S.V.P.":

"No, thank you."

The invitation was passed around at the party and became legendary.

One evening a few years later, when I was in eighth grade, I went around the neighborhood with my father measuring knee reflexes. It was my project for science class. Nana refused; I had to lift Mrs. Kent's long dress up above her knee; after the Farnys we asked each other whether we should knock on the strange couple's door.

"Why not?" said my father. "For a laugh."

Without him at my side I never would have, but there we were, knocking, the porch light came on, the door opened.

It was a thirty-year-old man wearing a T-shirt and thick glasses. He was unshaven, his hair was black and curly.

"We're from the neighborhood," explained my father.

"Nice to meet you," replied the young man, sticking out his hand. "We've just moved in."

And that is how we learned that the family nobody knew had moved away.

One summer Mr. Manson painted one side of his white house pink. But he did not paint that one side completely. Near the top of the gable, where his ladder didn't quite reach—if he had stood on the last rung and stretched he could have managed—was ever visible a triangular splotch of the old coat. When three years later the Mansons moved to Omaha, three sides of the house were finished, but the back remained a dusty, chippy white; in a few places whole sections of paint had peeled. We never did get to know the new neighbors, but the first thing they did was to paint the house all over again, this time beige.

When it came to tuning up cars, though, Mr. Manson couldn't have been more meticulous. He would put his bare hands under the hood and push and tug and twist, ensuring that all the caps and valves and wires and belts were tight and taut. He would clean, then oil everything that whirled and stroked. Racing the engine, then letting it idle, he would step to one side of the hood, then to the other, putting his ear to the motor. His garage contained heaps of spare parts and tools and tires, so much junk that there was no room for his own car. So Mr. Manson's old Chevy, which purred like a Cadillac, slept outside, covered winter and summer alike with a canvas tarp three times too big which he had purchased at the Army Surplus Store.

All the fathers in the neighborhood took their cars to Mr. Manson whenever the oil or the spark plugs needed changing. Mr. Manson also gave check-ups. All weekend long we would see him out on his driveway working over somebody's car, though usually he was under it, on a dolly. Whenever he emerged he would take on a reprimanding air, his raised eyebrow and head-shaking saying it all, even without the technical explications which concluded thus:

"Shit! If you had waited another week, I wouldn't have been able to save her!"

My father would reach for his wallet and try to pay him.

Mr. Manson would refuse.

My father would insist.

"Okay, okay," Mr. Manson would say, yielding. "Treat me to a beer or two."

That was the fee and a six-pack of Schlitz was always in the refrigerator, chilling. Off the two men would go. Mr. Manson's wife Mary, a tiny woman whose face was perpetually flushed, the mother of their five children, a devout Catholic, prohibited Big Leonard to drink in the house. Mr. Manson would beat his wife, as he did his children (especially his namesake, Little Leonard), and often the commotion boomed out the open windows of their house to reverberate throughout the neighborhood. But when it came to liquor, Mr. Manson lived in holy terror of his wife. He would down a half-dozen beers out on our patio, then reach into his pocket for a packet of mint breath fresheners.

Mr. Manson worked as a shoe salesman at Younkers Department Store, a job usually filled by high-school students working part-time. Why he didn't work in a garage or in a body shop as a mechanic puzzled many, but not my mother, who maintained:

"It boils down to this. He wants to wear a tie."

My mother liked shopping in the evening, and Younkers

stayed open until nine. But we avoided the shoe department.

"Are we going to say hello to Mr. Manson?" I inquired once or twice, but my mother, taking my hand, replied:

"Some other time."

Mr. Manson, Ernie, Steve Boyce and Jimmy Cellini were the neighborhood personnages from whose influence my mother strove to shield me. It is true that I was afraid of Mr. Manson, but not just because he beat his children, my playmates. He looked cruel. He was tall and lanky, with sinewy arms dangling out of his sleeveless T-shirts. He had a low forehead, and thinning, brillcreamed hair combed backwards, tight to the scalp. On the weekends Mr. Manson didn't shave.

I never learned what happened to him.

Entering the house one autumn afternoon, a year or two after the Mansons had moved away, I found my mother and Mrs. Manson talking in the living room. On her lap was perched a drooling baby, one obviously born since their departure. I strode over and greeted her warmly, asking about Diana and Little Leonard. But there were tears in Mrs. Manson's eyes. My mother sent me off on a long errand.

That evening at dinner, while the meat loaf and au gratin potatoes were being passed around, I noticed my mother wanted to say something. She began a sentence, she cleared her throat, then another thought came to her mind:

"Mary Manson is moving back to Des Moines."

"Oh really?" said my father. "Why?"

"We'll talk about it later," she replied, nodding over towards me.

Every now and then I catch myself thinking of what to buy my mother for a present. The lights strung across the street, the frost, the exhaust; I stop in front of a shopwindow and contemplate that red porcelain cup— Royal Albert "Lady Hamilton"—or on my way across town to meet Françoise remember that coffee pot I sent to my mother from Greece. It was a tin *briki*. Then I remember—the wind swirls, the buses roar by—that my mother has been dead for years.

I'm lost in such thoughts for seconds, minutes, then I remember.

That last vacation we all came, even my grandmother. One evening, as we were sitting around the dining-room table, my mother lowered her head. Tears fell, she pushed feebly against the table, she got up, she slowly left the room. Françoise said:

"Aren't you going to go with her?"

My father said:

"This happens."

We ate on in silence. Tips of forks touched china; someone sipped water; as always, my grandmother chewed too loudly, sighed. No one said a word though no one said a word....

In such noisy silences—every now and then—my mother lives.

Some said that she was from Yugoslavia, others that she was from Poland, but everybody agreed that she had fled from the Nazis, then from the Communists. On her legs were gruesome scars from the barbed wire. So said my mother, in any case. I never saw the scars. When Anna cleaned our house she wore a thin, dark-blue work dress that came down nearly to her ankles. She loved to talk, but spoke rapidly in an accent so thick that most of the time all we could do was smile. Sometimes Anna said something, then burst out laughing— a singsong laugh. We laughed with her. For my mother, Anna was in the same class as Dr. Hill, the pediatrician: "People too good to be true."

"Anna—what a godsend!" she would say, examining the linoleum floor. "She had to get down on her hands and knees and make a new life for herself."

"What do you mean?" I inquired.

"She came from one of the richest families in Yugoslavia. And I learned that she studied music at a conservatory in Vienna."

That Anna had studied music may have had some truth to it; her daughter Anna Maria, whom I never met though she was my age, studied the violin at school and won a prize. Anna's husband worked at the Firestone plant as a tire builder, but had been trained in Europe as a furniture maker.

"You wouldn't believe the tables and chairs they have in their house," recounted my mother that Christmas she and my father dropped off a box of homemade pralines.

"And the African violets," added my father.

Anna had special lights and soils and fertilizers, knew how to cross the plants and make hybrids. She was always bringing my mother little pots of them, explaining in her incomprehensible accent when to water, how much light they needed and especially when the violets needed to be divided. It was the dividing of the African violets that panicked my mother. Every other time that Anna came my mother would ask whether the plants were big enough.

"Not yet," Anna would reply, then touch the soil with her thick, chafed index finger. "But no more water, you know."

I do not know how Ruth and Ernie came across Anna, who lived on the south side of Des Moines, but when Ruth received her promotion at the Telephone Company they had their house repainted and hired her. Not too long afterwards Anna started coming to our house too, every Wednesday.

But what exactly did Anna clean? Every Tuesday evening—after the dishes were done—out of the closet came the dust rags, the sponges, the Ajax, the vacuum cleaner; my father emptied the wastepaper baskets, took out the trash; my mother started scrubbing in the kitchen. Ann, Joan and I were responsible for the den, the living room; once they were put in order we attacked our own rooms, stuffing wads of clothes in dresser drawers, picking up our books. Before leaving for school the next morning our beds had to be made, the toothpaste in the bathroom sink washed away. Anna usually drove up just as we were walking down 48th Street.

"Kids, hi!" she shouted, waving from the driver's seat.

Anna completed the housecleaning chores in a precise order, beginning with the upstairs bathroom, finishing with the ironing in the basement. During school vacations we had to be up and out of our rooms by eight; often my mother arranged for early doctor's or dentist's appointments followed by errands and lunch downtown so that the house would be completely free. Once the kitchen floor had been waxed, we couldn't go to the refrigerator for at least two hours; Anna placed a chair in each doorway. She used Ajax for the toilet, scrubbed the inside walls with a long-handled brush, then left the gray, effervescent liquid standing in the bowl. My mother always flushed the toilet immediately after cleaning it, so whenever Anna had left the liquid standing I was unsure when it was permissible to urinate. Sometimes I could retain myself no longer, would urinate, then pull down the lid, ever so softly touch the trip handle so that only a little water would be released, keeping the noise to a minimum. From behind my bedroom door I then listened for Anna's footsteps. But she never came to check, never said a word. I eventually asked my mother why Anna did things that way.

My mother gave me a questioning look, as if I were perhaps not yet old enough to know.

Finally she replied:

"I think it's because in Poland the water was so expensive that flushing the toilet for nothing was almost a luxury."

My mother would fix Anna's lunch and during the fifteen years that she cleaned our house Anna never requested, to my knowledge, but the following menu: a glass of milk, a bowl of chicken-noodle soup, potato chips, and a tuna-fish sandwich made with two unbuttered slices of white bread.

"But wouldn't she like something else for change?" I asked my mother one day that year I was living at home. "A tossed salad? A grilled cheese sandwich?"

I had started to like cooking and even suggested that we sauté some vegetables.

But when I went to ask Anna she only laughed, then turned the vacuum cleaner back on.

I stood there for a moment; Anna again turned off the vacuum cleaner.

"Why go you in Europe?" she cried, waving her hefty forearm in protest, "when you can live in America!"

By July I was gone for good. I never saw Anna again.

A year or so after my mother died my father let Anna go.

"The remarriage would have been hard on her," he explained. "She was so attached to your mother."

Thereafter Anna stopped working entirely. Her son had finally finished college; her daughter, the musician, was working, thanks to Ruth, for the Telephone Company. Her husband was about to retire.

"They're planning a trip to Florida," added my father, "with the retirement bonus. Anna said they hadn't been a day out of town in nearly forty years."

"I'll give her a call the next time I'm home."

Six years passed, but I remembered. When I asked my father for the number, he paused; so I said:

"Find it tomorrow."

I took an orange from the refrigerator, peeled it. We sat down at the kitchen table.

It was exactly four o'clock in the afternoon.

I knew that I should change the subject. What was the use of bringing up my mother? What was the use of bringing up Anna? I gazed out a nearby window. A worker was repairing a roof; to the left was a park in which I had sometimes played as a child: Greenwood Park.

"What a view you have," I remember saying.

We talked about the Art Center for a while: hundreds of thousands of dollars had been spent to buy a canvas covered with bright red paint; taxpayers from all over Iowa had written in protest to the *Des Moines Register*.

"Do you remember the Arman show?" I asked.

I reminded my father of the smashed-up violins in plexiglas.

My father wasn't paying attention. He looked at me and said:

"Sometimes I wonder whether we should have paid Anna more than we did."

Every three weeks or so I had my hair cut at Whitey's Barbershop, located alongside the entrance to the McNeil Motel, across Urbandale Avenue from St. Andrew's Episcopal Church. There was a sort of shopping center located around the motel: Richard's Pharmacy, an insurance agent's office or two, a tavern, a beauty salon, and Heaven to Seven, a children's clothing store which eventually expanded and added to its sign: "Now with Sizes to Fourteen!"

Back then the city limits of Des Moines ran along the western edge of this group of shops, the boundary drawn up the center of Merle Hay Road, which was in fact Highway 401. Thus Whitey had for customers, besides the fathers and sons who lived in those one-story houses at the bottom of Urbandale Avenue—from 53rd Street, say, down to 59th—, traveling salesmen from the small towns in Iowa, traveling salesmen who arrived in Des Moines for a day or two, lodged at the McNeil Motel, with station wagons full of paint samples, catalogs, encyclopedias, gadgets of all kinds, sporting goods, men with worn suits, with cigarettes in their mouths, men who hunted and fished, took in a ball game when they could, men always full of news from the radio stations.

When I started going to Whitey's there were two other barbers, Milhaud, his partner—the shop was in fact called "White & Milhaud's"—and always a third fellow, young, chubby, shy, just graduated from the Barber's College, who usually moved on after a while, sometimes to open his own shop in Waukee or Grimes, sometimes to quit barbering completely, to work in a grocery store or go into his father-in-law's real estate business.

Mike was like that, though he stayed on longer than most. Long after he had quit, Mike still dropped in on Saturday mornings, slimmed down, sporting a blue blazer and a pinstripe shirt, his cufflinks showing, freshly shaved, a new man.

"How's things, Mr. White?" he would grin, bursting in, Whitey setting down his clippers and shaking his hand warmly, Milhaud grunting something.

"Great, Mike, and the kids?"

Everything came to a halt while Mike went on about the luck he had had, never really giving the details, but with such excitement and optimism in his voice that the men standing slapped him on the back, those sitting wishing him even more success the next time—"Go out and get 'em, Mike," "Keep it up, tiger"—before chipping in with their own stories, the pheasant season, the Yankees, Johnny Unitas, the horses in Omaha.

"Well, we'd all better get back to work," he would at last interrupt, shaking hands all around, waving goodbye. "Got to see a fellow this morning at the State-house."

Out the door Mike would go, Whitey shaking his head in admiration, the others beginning to express their envy, the bad breaks they had had, someone rising:

"Get a load of that car!"

At just that moment Mike would give a parting beep-beep, then drive off in his new Chevrolet.

At Whitey's, whenever one of the three barbers became free, the next customer in line had to get up and
go over to him, even if that meant a botched job by
the Barber's College graduate or the one hairstyle of
which Milhaud was capable, one very closely resem-
bling his own. I hated it whenever my hair got under
Milhaud's shears. He had a rough manner, gripped
the top of the head with one strong hand, ran the overheated
clippers so close to the scalp around the ears that it
burned. In addition he was unpleasant, always in a
bad mood, the weight of the world on his slumping
shoulders. Tall, gangling, with a lot of bone jutting
out around his eyes, Milhaud swore constantly.

One Saturday morning I was after the man next-in-
line when Milhaud's chair became free.

I continued leafing through my *Sports Illustrated.*

But then the man jabbed my arm with his elbow.

"Go ahead, son, I'll wait for Whitey."

Milhaud muttered a curse, then ordered me up into
his chair. He draped the sheet around my chest and
shoulders; when he tightened the collar he nearly choked
me.

Times were changing, so were hairstyles. When the
third barber left the shop for a car-selling job in Marshalltown,
Whitey and Milhaud did not replace him. The regular
customers began joking about the long hair that was
becoming the fashion among the junior-high and high-
school boys.

"Just wait," said Whitey, gesturing with his comb.
"It's going to kill the barbering business."

"Send 'em all to Vietnam, I say," sneered Milhaud,
and in a chorus of "You bet's" and "That'd show 'em's,"
all those fathers and traveling salesmen agreed.

Whitey didn't say a word. From the look in his eyes,

from the renewed concentration with which he trimmed the sideburn, I could tell that he was truly worried. Back then, at least during the baseball and basketball seasons, I kept my hair in a crewcut.

But even such men as sat in Whitey's Barbershop began paying attention to their hairstyles. The number of customers waiting for Whitey increased. It got to the point that on some Saturday mornings Milhaud, abandoning his chair, went down to the soda fountain at Richard's for a cup of coffee while four or five men sat around talking shotguns or the World Series and waiting for Whitey. Whitey was embarrassed; he blushed easily anyway. Sometimes he also took a break, saying to the waiting men:

"Hey, fellows. One or two of you go with Milhaud. I've got an errand to run before noon."

But the men waited. They knew that Whitey had only gone down to Richard's to have a prescription filled or to pick up some cough drops.

Luckily there were newcomers, men who stuck their heads in the doorway and said:

"Oh, I see you're busy."

"A little," Milhaud would retort, climbing out of his chair, setting his magazine down on the windowsill. "But I can work you in right now."

As for myself, I observed what was happening, but for at least a year did not know whether I too could "wait for Whitey." I was thirteen years old. I rode my bike to Whitey's. Often when I arrived he asked "how the ol' pitchin' arm was," then gestured towards Milhaud. How could anyone like Milhaud? How could anyone be satisfied with the haircut he gave? But how could anyone not feel sorry for him, the barbershop packed

with men chatting away, fathers and traveling salesmen, every single last one of them waiting for Whitey?
Then one morning only one customer was ahead of
me when I came in. Milhaud leapt to his feet, but I,
hanging up my jacket, said:

"I'd like to wait for Mr. White, please."

Milhaud let out a string of cusswords, ripped off his
protective blouse, without a word stormed out of the
shop, slammed the door behind him. Whitey looked at
me, not really angry—exhausted.

I'm not sure whether I saw Milhaud again. About
that time he quit; Whitey, making great sacrifices, bought
his share of the partnership, ran thereafter the shop
by himself, did not hire a new barber since all along
business had been falling off anyway, the traveling salesmen
now needing an easy-going, youthful appearance that
Whitey did not know how to give. What did Whitey
know about blow-driers and hair spray for men? He
did remove the soft-drink machine from the back room
and install separate shampooing facilities, repaint the
shop, buy new light fixtures and a carpet, try to famil-
iarize himself with all the new hairstyling gadgets. He
took down the traditional sign of the barbershop, the
rotating red and white pole, redid the lettering on the
front window. But by the time Whitey had more or
less learned how to trim long hair—with a razor—a
new generation of hair stylists was giving carefully
scissored haircuts with shampooing, blow-drying and
hair spray included, the fee sometimes even compris-
ing a shoulder massage. I remained faithful as long as
possible, till the end of my last basketball season. Then
I too let my hair grow.

Two or three years later, while home for Christmas

vacation, I ran into Whitey at Merle Hay Plaza.

"I've got them both in college!" he exclaimed shaking my hand, referring to his children, one of whom, Susan, had been in my homeroom in high school.

"That's great, Mr. White," I replied.

We talked for a while; Whitey asked me what I was studying; he spoke about my old high-school basketball team.

"What ever happened to Dick Wittenbroodt?" he inquired.

"As far as I know, he's still at the Air Force Academy."

"Oh no," replied Whitey. "I don't think so."

Finally we said good-bye. I told him to give my best to Susan.

Two or three days passed.

One morning after breakfast, on the spur of the moment, I asked my mother for the keys to the car.

"Where are you going?" she asked.

"Don't worry about it," I replied.

She gave me a hurt look, but without a further word I put on my coat.

"I'm going to surprise you with something," I said as I was leaving.

I closed the door leading to the garage, got in the car, turned on the radio, backed down the driveway.

The streets were covered with a crunchy layer of packed snow. Not a neighbor was out; everything was frozen.

I headed towards Whitey's Barbershop, driving through familiar side streets, turned down Urbandale Avenue, nearly pulled into the parking lot, but at the last instant drove on.

When the last Reed's Ice Cream Shop was transformed into a clothing store—just after the summer that Rachel worked there—a period of history came to a close. First downtown Des Moines was razed, then rebuilt. Merle Hay Plaza, the shopping center, expanded. Other shopping centers were built, two in West Des Moines, another to the south of town. A new kind of ice cream shop appeared, in fact not a shop but a store—a factory— located no longer in the small neighborhood shopping districts but on the outskirts of town, where Hickman Road became Highway 6 for example, a neon-lit ice cream store with no place to sit down, with music blaring from the speakers, with long lines to stand in before being served, with sleepy high-school kids in raspberry and licorice-stained aprons scooping up the lime with the dipper they had just used for the apricot, with families eating cones in cars as if at a drive-in movie, with scores of "natural" flavors that tasted like thawed syrup, too sweet, too runny, holes ever in the bottom of those cones, a mess!

How different Reed's was! At the Reed's on Beaver Avenue Mrs. Johannsen knew all the children by name, who played baseball and who played the violin, who had received straight A's and who had had his tonsils out, who had run away and who went to church. On summer evenings families would drop in while taking a walk. After an Open House or the Christmas Program at school Reed's was packed; a sundae was the reward for a good report card, a Little League victory, chores completed. Any Saturday morning, afternoon, evening, any day after school until five, Reed's was crowded, full of light, full of conversation.

The three Reed's Ice Cream Shops were associated with everyone's adolescent, even adult love life. After Mr. Dimitrion's divorce, it was at the Franklin Avenue shop that my father and I dropped him off after baseball practice—so he could meet a friend. At the same shop, years later, I would sit at the counter working through a hot fudge sundae while Rachel served the other customers. From time to time there was a lull; we would try to talk, till Rachel's boss, a pale, middle-aged lady who bunched her wig into an enormous sanitary net, told her to sponge down the milk-shake machine or to restack the takeout cartons. I was always impressed by Rachel's retorts:

"I'll get it done."

She would turn to me, raise her eyes to the ceiling, we would talk a moment more.

It was with Debbie, six years earlier, that I went to the Reed's on Forest Avenue for the first time. It was three times larger than the other two shops—long, narrow, with huge fans stirring the air from above. Debbie and I felt ill at ease with so many college students around; before the waitress came we left, then walked home, hand in hand, through unknown neighborhoods: Clark Avenue, Witmer Park, Marella Drive. Our mothers each thought we were with friends at the Drake Relays.

The year before, when I was in sixth grade, I needed permission to stop at the Reed's in Beaverdale on my way home from school. Six or seven of us would crowd into a booth, order milk shakes, ice cream. Invariably I asked Mrs. Johannsen for three scoops of banana. Dan and Dick would position me on the end; but not once did Janine, across from us, look over. Tall, thin, athletic, the smartest girl in class, she was also the cutest. Years later, seniors in high school, we sat next to each other in physics. No longer the cutest, no longer the smartest, not even an athlete, Janine had in the meantime lost Janine. What ever happened to her? Sometimes I think of that bland, unsmiling face hers had become— never without an intimation of tragedy.

It was at the end of that same year that I had my first date, not with Janine, but with Annie. Notes had been exchanged; now, returning from recess on the last day of school, I found another note in my desk.

I looked across the classroom. Annie, neither smiling nor frowning, was staring at me through the light-blue, spangled frames of her glasses.

I nodded; at the door, at the end of the period, I whispered:

"Three-thirty."

Then I raced to the parking lot, hopped on my bike, tore down Urbandale Avenue to 48th Street. Arriving home, I burst in the back way, let my books drop on the kitchen table, told my mother there was a football game back at school.

"Thanks for coming home to tell me," she said.

I sped towards Reed's—New York Avenue, 42nd Street, Sheridan Avenue—parked my bicycle outside, went in, found an empty booth. Mrs. Johannsen came over:

"What'll you have, Johnny?"

"Do you mind, Mrs. Johannsen," I asked, "if I order in a minute or two? I'm expecting a friend."

Mrs. Johannsen bent down and whispered through a cloud of perfume:

"What's her name?"

I began waiting. From time to time I glanced at the clock behind the counter: 3:25, 3:30, 3:35, 3:40, 3:45:...

Suddenly I panicked. I stood up, went over to the counter, got Mrs. Johannsen's attention, ordered a chocolate sundae covered with marshmallow sauce. She looked at me strangely, but without a word started scooping out the ice cream. In a moment she brought the sundae over to my booth.

"What's wrong? She stand you up?"

Just as I was finishing the sundae Annie arrived. She sat right down, full of excitement, blushing a little, glanced at my empty ice cream dish.

"Annie," I said, completely ashamed of myself, "I went ahead and ordered."

"Oh," she replied.

By now Reed's was full; I had trouble getting Mrs. Johannsen to come back over. Annie kept saying she didn't want anything.

"But I want you to have the same thing I had," I pleaded.

Finally Mrs. Johannsen arrived, all hustle, bustle; a tray loaded down with glasses, dishes; her face flushed....

"What'll it be?" she demanded, giving Annie a ferocious look.

Annie ordered a Diet Pepsi.

As we were leaving I realized how stupid I was to have ridden my bicycle. Annie still had her books and folders; etiquette required that I carry them home for her. So, taking them under my left arm, I endeavored to push the bicycle along with my right hand, switching as well whenever necessary to the street side of the sidewalk. Annie talked about her brother.

"He says that in junior high you have to study a lot. This summer he's going to Ames for basketball camp. He's going to be an engineer...."

At the corner of 45th Street and Beavercrest Drive I stopped, unsure whether I should walk Annie all the way to her front door. Were her parents home? She lived towards the middle of 45th Street, a shadowy street lined with parked cars, a street which seemed to funnel into a dead end, a street which I had avoided even before I knew her. Annie said:

"We'll probably see each other this summer."

She reached out for her books.

"If you want," I replied, handing them over, "you can come and watch my baseball games."

Not once did I see Annie that summer. June. July. Often I rode my bicycle around those streets. Beavercrest, Holcomb, Sheridan, New York Avenue, 44th Street, 46th Street. Warming up before our games, I would look over at the stands, hoping that she had come. But they had built new fields for us out of town, all the way out Beaver Avenue towards Johnston. I kept telling myself that Annie had no way of getting there. In August we left for Idaho.

All that summer I was in love with Annie Peterson. I thought of her constantly; one day I confessed everything to my sisters.

"What does she look like?" they asked.

I didn't want to tell them. Annie Peterson was a feeling.

Came at last the end of summer.

Came at last the first day of school.

She turned up in my algebra class. We talked at the door; she seemed distant, embarrassed; when the bell rang and Mr. Crookshank arrived she hurried away, to the far side of the classroom; just one seat was free.

Dejected, I sat down at the nearest table, next to a girl I didn't know. Mr. Crookshank started calling out our names. Towards the end he came to the name of the girl sitting next to me. She repeated it several times for him; it was a tongue twister. Some of the students were laughing. I was only half-listening. What could I care what her name was? All I wanted was Annie. I stared at the varnished wood of the tabletop, at a name freshly engraved there. What had I done? What had happened? Was there someone else?... Slowly, amidst the laughter and commotion, I turned in my seat to search out Annie's eyes.

On his last trip to Paris my father brought my old identity bracelet to me. The house had been sold, the drawers of my dresser cleaned out; with the bracelet came my high-school wristwatch and a few things belonging to my mother.

"What about that photograph of Leon Hook?" I asked, referring to a distant cousin, long dead, whose short life had become a family legend.

"I don't remember seeing that in your stuff," he replied.

For months the identity bracelet lay on my desk, covered with clippings, papers, receipts. I found it again while cleaning. I picked it up, Françoise came over, I handed it to her. She started examining it.

"Why is it so marked up?" she asked.

We were tired of cleaning the house, we sat down in the living room.

I spoke about the past.

I told her about how we used to give identity bracelets to girlfriends. I told her what "going steady" meant. Then we ate dinner.

After dinner I found a way to hang the identity bracelet from my desk lamp. There it hangs still.

Every now and then, while sitting at my desk, I am overcome by an indefinite feeling, somehow sad, somehow fearful. My fingers search for objects, a ball-point pen, a paper clip, the Scotch tape. And sometimes I take down the identity bracelet, start playing with the clasp, even put it on and wear it for a while.

We met because Geoff and Mike thought we ought to meet. Anne was tall, timid; she studied the flute, liked Saint-Saëns, Edgar Varèse. On our first date I waited a good half hour in the foyer before she came down. She handed me a record for Geoff. In the Student Union Anne rarely looked up from her coffee, blushed constantly; when she laughed her hand rose to her mouth like a child. I called the next day: we went to see *The Paper Chase*.

Our third date was to the new restaurant on the outskirts of town. Mike and Mary came too; Mike ordered the wine; there was an ice bucket, candles burning on the table. Anne didn't say a word. Mary talked about her parents, music came softly from the speakers, a professor I knew came in. When Anne and Mary went to the rest room Mike looked at me; I shrugged my shoulders; but as we were walking out of the restaurant, behind Mike and Mary, Anne took my hand.

On Monday I skipped class, ran across campus to hear her recital. I stood outside the door, listened to cellos, then oboes, bassoons. Where was the harpsicord that was supposed to accompany her?

Suddenly Anne was beside me. She burst out laughing, blushed, her hand covered her mouth, she was obviously ill at ease.

Her turn had been moved up to three-thirty.

We hurriedly said good-bye; she had a test to take; leaving, I gave her shoulder a caress.

"Way to go!" announced Geoff when he came in that

evening. "She couldn't believe you came!"

"Did she say how her test went?"

Mike arrived, we stayed up talking well past midnight.

I began surprising her. I showed up at noon to walk her to class; once I even came at ten, with the book she wanted, checked out of the library.

"I thought you might like this one as well."

I held out a thin volume.

Anne looked at me, shook her head, smiled, reached to my cheek with her fingers. Even at that point she would remain silent; her silences moved and bewildered me; another week went by; I sought every excuse to see her.

We took long walks, across the town, around the campus. Gradually she spoke about the past, her father, San Francisco. One evening she told me how the boys at school had called her "Horse."

"Because of my hips," she said. "And I'm so flat-chested."

She took my hand in hers, lifted it to her breast. She smiled, but her thoughts, her gaze, seemed faraway. Was she sad? I put my arm around her, kissed her cheek. Under a streetlight we stopped and embraced.

The next morning, her birthday, I sent to Anne a dozen roses.

She didn't call. The morning, the afternoon, the evening passed. Towards nine I called, myself. She wasn't in.

I walked to the Music Building, came to the stairs leading to the practice rooms. I never bothered her there; she had asked me not to. Down the stairs I went. Through one of the padded doors I heard her playing. I listened for a moment; I was afraid to turn the doorknob; I left.

I went back and wrote out a message: "Dropped by around 9:30. You must be practicing. Call when you're finished, even if it's after midnight."

For two days I waited.

Like the first time, Anne kept me waiting for at least a half hour in the foyer before she came down. Christie entered, waved a hello, ran up the stairs. For a while I stood next to a window, then sat down, leafed through a textbook which someone had left on the coffee table. Anne joined me there.

Two months later, just a few days before I left for Des Moines (and, a year later, for Europe), I ran into Anne in a deserted corridor of the Administration Building. She said hello, kept walking past, I stopped her.

"I still don't understand," I said.

She said nothing. She looked at me as if I had hurt her, then turned away, walked away.

My eyes followed her out the door, across the lawn.

It was early summer. Everything was still, bathed in the pale rays of the morning sun. I saw Anne putting her arms through the sleeves of her sweater, she strangely clapped her hands in front of her, then she started running.

When my father telephoned that my maternal grandmother had died, I thought of the time she took me down-town on the bus to have poached pike in that diner near Younkers Department Store. I couldn't understand why my mother wasn't coming. I was told to put on my parka, my overshoes. Then my mother bent down and kissed me good-bye. Without saying a word she pulled the hood over my head, tied the drawstrings. Grandma led me out the front door, we started down the driveway, step by step, Grandma holding onto my arm, down 48th Street we went, down the bobsled hill, to Urbandale Avenue.

We waited a long time for the bus to come. It was a still, sunless, snowless day, not a sign of life, not a stir, the air brittle, freezing like a pane of glass. I blew hot air from the back of my throat, the gray flame of the dragon.

"Johnny," said my grandmother, "you put the money in."

I released the quarters through the slot of the metal box.

In the diner a white-jacketed waiter brought over the steaming fish. My grandmother asked about the potatoes, the cup of coffee. Then she picked up her knife and fork, cut the flesh back from around the bones. She reached across the table.

"Grandma," I asked, "is this fish from the ocean?"

The flesh was light, white, spongy. I chewed it, kept chewing it, swallowed. Then I drank some water. I looked over at my grandmother. In my ears rang the distant echo of her reply, that pike was freshwater fish.

"Have you finished your meal, Johnny?" she asked.

She scrutinized me with her wide, intimidating eyes, then added:

"Your mother doesn't care for fish. Next time we come downtown we'll try some trout. Just the two of us, like today."

We spent the afternoon browsing in Younkers. Gloves, scarves, kitchen appliances, then candy, then girdles. My grandmother pronounced the word in front of me.

"Wait here," she said, "I'm going to pay for these girdles."

She waddled off towards the girl at the cash register. The crowd of Christmas shoppers flowed around her; I strained to follow her with my eyes; she vanished.

She has vanished.

"I'll do something," I said. "I'll write a letter to Bob and John."

"That would be nice," said my father.

And as he told me about his trip home, I thought about the weight she gained when my grandfather got Parkinson's disease, the fifteen years she nursed him, day in, day out, with only those rare trips to Des Moines for escape, my grandmother, who after every long separation never failed to ask—it broke the silence, changed the subject—whether I still remembered the day she had taken me downtown on the bus to have poached pike in that diner near Younkers Department Store.

The other day, while copying addresses and telephone numbers out of an old address book into a new one, I came to my grandmother's name. She had died a few years back, but whenever leafing through the W's I had refrained from crossing out her name and address. The summers we spent there; the letters I had sent to that address:

"In camp having fun!"

"Tomorrow is another day."

I was six years old.

It was a small white house with a tiny lawn. A front walk, two front steps. On each side juniper bushes. In front of them a row of marigolds. Behind the window on the right my grandfather's room. Helen who came to take care of him, her son who had been in prison.

Stuttering Elmer who with his hand mower cut the spongy grass.

Elmer's overalls, Elmer's muscular hands, Elmer's smell: sweat, cold chicken, lubricating oil.

These are my memories, these memories will remain.

Can it matter that I decided to turn the page, to copy Dimitri's name, address and two telephone numbers, one for his office, one for his home?

On the way to the bakery yesterday I came across a group of people watching an old lady and her bulldog. She was wearing a stained overcoat; her hair was uncombed; the bulldog was standing there motionlessly, its legs apart, while the old lady, bent over behind it, was caressing its penis and bladder so it could urinate. The urine trickled down from the penis, wet the sidewalk, eventually formed a rivulet which pooled around the dog's right forepaw. The dog didn't move; only its mouth opened slightly from time to time while it panted, then closed. The woman, continuing to stroke the animal, was whispering something to it or perhaps she was only speaking to herself. I couldn't really tell. Besides, the people around me were laughing and a middle-aged woman with dyed blond hair was shouting out advice. I turned away from the spectacle, crossed the boulevard, walked towards the bakery. I was in a hurry.

On the way back I found the old lady and the bulldog alone, the dog lying at her feet, the woman sitting on a stone parapet and leaning back against the screen fence which rose above it. Suddenly the métro roared out of the tunnel just below.

When the noise subsided I asked:

"Votre chien, Madame, ça va?"

The woman looked away—into the wind. I decided not to trouble her further.

But the dog, its head resting on its paws, was gazing at my shoes; it looked up at me. There is no ending to this story.

I apologize for the Greek, but years back I had learned the language, even some slang, and "Mangissa" fit perfectly the tall, muscular girl with the narrow eyes and massive jaw who sold fruits and vegetables outside the Radar grocery store on the avenue de Choisy. So "Mangissa" we nicknamed her. Whether she had contacts in the Parisian underworld we never did learn, but she wore tight jeans, high-heeled boots and even on balmy spring afternoons a sleeveless black-leather jacket whose bulging pockets concealed mysterious objects...in any case packs of those malodorous *Gauloises* she kept between her lips while bagging up tomatoes and punching the grimy keys of the cash register. At the foot of the cash register, which stood on two wobbly fruit crates, lay with black eyes open the German shepherd which every day accompanied Mangissa from her dive (or so we imagined) in the 20th arrondissement, through several long corridors of the Métro, to the place d'Italie. The dog sometimes got up when a customer was paying, sniffed about his legs, even forcibly pushing him back and growling as if to protect her.

Tough as she looked, Mangissa also had that sad smile of those gritty dames in the thirties who married boxers and sang poignant songs in cabarets. More than once I saw her slip an apple to one of the bums from the Centre Nicolas-Flamel; with old ladies she would lose patience, but the very poorest among them, the ones half out of their minds who wore filthy raincoats and toted about plastic sacks full of old clothes, must never have paid for their two potatoes. The other girls who worked at Radar not only tended a cash register but also had to stock the shelves and mop the aisles. Even Tête-à-Gifles sometimes had to mop the floor. But not once, I am sure, did Mangissa ever squeeze a *serpillière* out over a bucket. Even on the harshest winter mornings, when the fruit stand was moved inside, Mangissa never condescended to tasks so lowly. Surely the manager, an alcoholic of about fifty with a limp and a breathless, raspish voice, was afraid of her and of *who might be her friends*. At precisely ten minutes before closing time Mangissa stacked the crates into piles of three and hefted them, with less effort than one had expected, inside. Only her very favorite customers, arriving on the run at '7:13, had a chance of talking her into reaching into one of those crates for a box of strawberries or a lemon. You paid the price she announced and the money—even when the manager was looking—went straight into her pocket.

I admit that in time and indeed in spite of myself I too became one of Mangissa's favorite customers. We like everyone else had been shortchanged by her once or twice, but back then Radar had, if one excepted the mushy zucchinis and the woody leeks, the best fruits and vegetables in the quarter. The strawberries and the mandarin oranges were especially delicious. They had the freshest lettuce. So when we discovered that we had paid, the day before, 117 francs for a kilo of tomatoes—Mangissa must have made a mint off the 200-franc notes that had just been issued—we kept going to her anyway, deciding not to boycott the store as we had done in so many similar cases, only henceforth resolved to carefully count out our change. It strikes me now that Mangissa in fact became friendly to us only then, after we had started counting out our change in front of her. One day she asked Françoise where I was from. From that day on Mangissa called me "Monsieur John."

The appellation brought with it privileges. When I arrived at the end of the line at six o'clock on a Friday afternoon Mangissa would, if no other favorite customers were present, serve me first, calling me forward with such authority in her deep, monotonic voice that not one of the other women—strangers or newcomers to the quarter—dared to protest. She gave me the best fruits or let me pick them out myself. If I needed a plastic sack she always had one stashed behind the stand—and I mean one of those thick plastic sacks with broad, sturdy handles. No matter how busy she was, and suddenly in a commiserate tone, Mangissa would ask about Françoise:

"Monsieur John, is your wife all right?..."

More than by anything else, even my accent, Mangissa was intrigued by the fact that it was I who nearly always did the shopping.

"She isn't sick, is she?..."

I explained to Mangissa that everything was fine, that I worked at home, that it was easier for me to take care of the shopping than for Françoise, who commuted to work.

Mangissa stared at me with her dark, narrow eyes, nodded her head reflectively; she wanted to be understanding, that I could see, but the arrangement greatly troubled her.

Her private life remained a mystery. Once by chance I saw her driving a beaten-up Peugeot down the rue St-Louis-en-l'Ile, rapidly but with her left arm resting on the window, accompanied by the same girl—I am nearly sure it was the same girl—who sometimes stood talking and smoking cigarettes with her at the fruit stand, a girl of similar attributes, peroxided hair, heavy eye shadow, wearing a sequined jean jacket and around her neck a studded leather band little different from a dog collar. Whenever that girl was around, Mangissa remained aloof, even rude, a participant in some somber world of which I often sought to imagine the constituents.

It was not Mangissa but Débilette who told me that all of them were going to be transferred to the gigantic Radar supermarket near the place des Fêtes.

"The thought of leaving the quar...," she droned in her emotionless voice, letting her sentence trail off as was her custom, her eyes gazing beyond me and the other customers in line, beyond the cheeses and the yogurts, perhaps towards that tiny studio on the avenue Edison where on Sunday afternoons she sometimes sat on the windowsill, a pitiful dress on, her hair half done up, her knees slightly uncovered so as to receive the last slanting rays of the rare Parisian sun.

I held out a 10-franc coin to Débilette and in a moment she turned to me and took it.

A week or two passed.

I didn't go out of my way to say good-bye to Mangissa— so often in my life I have just slipped away, disappeared or let others disappear without leaving a trace.... But, as it turned out, I did end up at the fruit stand on her very last day.

"Monsieur John," she said as I stopped in front of her, "we're leaving."

"Yes, I know," I replied, noticing that she too was now wearing a dog collar. "The other girl told me. But when?"

"Today."

"I'm sorry about that."

"Yeah, so am I."

I asked Mangissa for a kilo of something or other, then for something else, then for something else again.

"Would you like anything else?" she inquired.

"No, no. That's all."

After I had paid I stood there for a moment, looking down the street, searching for something nice to say.

"I'll come up and see you at the place des Fêtes!" I remarked in a moment, hating myself immediately for making one more promise which I had little intention of keeping.

Mangissa smiled, we shook hands.

"I'll be waiting!"

But surely she knew as well as I did that we would never, except by utter chance, see each other again.

Trucks rumbled past, towards Chinatown. Somewhere in the distance, the sound of a jackhammer.

I gripped my groceries.

Then Mangissa whispered:

"Good-bye, Monsieur John."

I had been there twice, but by now so many years had gone by that I had to ask the girl in the office where it was. She gave me a concerned look, and I felt embarrassed, then she opened a large register. She confirmed the first name, looking up at me in the same way, then took a small card and wrote numbers on it. She handed me the card, a map, leaned over the counter; with the point of her pencil she showed me where the entrance was. Then she traced a line along the road I would have to follow.

"It will be right in here somewhere," she concluded, scribbling in a dot on the map. "Do you have a car?"

"No, I don't."

"Walking?"

"Yes."

I stood there for an instant, for I expected her to add something.

But she turned, sat down at the wooden table in the corner, picked up a small stack of bills, receipts, began sorting them. I left.

It was a sunny, chilly November morning. I walked around the outside of the office, crossed the parking lot, then headed down a winding road. Soon a pond appeared on the left, where two little girls and a man were trying to launch a paper boat. I watched them, knowing why they had come. One of the girls, upset about something, marched off; the man quickly left the other girl, ran after her.

The road twisted back in the other direction, entering a grove of trees. Tiny metal markers had been stuck in the ground; I took out the card, looked at it, then at the map, kept walking. Under my shirt and sweater I could feel the sweat cooling; I shivered. I had already walked from 39th and Grand, up Polk Boulevard, over the expressway. I zipped up my jacket, knotted my scarf. There was a little wind, a north wind.

In the distance workers, a truck; I heard the sound of a machine. Squirrels chasing each other, leaping from branch to branch. As I approached they froze, yet seemed to tremble; I slowed my pace so as not to frighten them.

Finally the sign I was looking for: "Block 29." I walked off the road, onto the grass.

Dead grass, soon to be covered by snow.

I now recognized everything. We had chosen the site because of the pine tree; there it was, not as tall as I had remembered, but broad, flat-topped, like a cedar. I thought of Lebanon, an automatic thought, a fact memorized at school, Franklin Junior High, just down the street, a fact for me as durable as my lifetime, a distracting fact which now brought relief.

I laughed to myself.

And there was the noise of the machine striking the earth, of workers shouting; a small bird darted past, up into the bare branches of a distant tree. All this is beautiful, I thought, death necessary for it to be so. At the same time I started crying.

I tried to pull myself together, to breathe deeply, an old habit. It was my mother who had taught me.

"When things get tight," she would say, "take a deep breath."

So I took one, gathered courage for the last steps.

The dead grass; the cold, spongy soil.
July 14, 1927–October 19, 1981. My mother's life.
I squatted over the damp, cold earth, reached out,
and gently touched her tiny marble grave.

Lying in bed at night my thoughts wander, I find myself anticipating a pain to come, in my heart, also in my penis, my testicles.

I fear such fears, for once as a boy faking a stomachache I found myself that very afternoon wheeled off to Surgery for an appendectomy. They had given me a sedative, but my mind was clear. I thought:

"I do feel pain."

The secret, kept from my parents forever, was that the pain, real in the end, was imagined into being.

Is it possible?

There had been examinations.

"We'll operate immediately," the doctor had said to my father. "It's acute."

There is sometimes a pain in my heart when I have walked fast and far. There is something strange in my right testicle. I lie in bed at night thinking of these things, the real pains, the anticipated ones, the thought that they are thoughts, the thought of what thoughts can do.

And I think of this:

I realized that day so long ago with what I said was a pain in my stomach, that I was no one else but myself.

I dreamt last night in German, of Christian. How long it had been since we had drunk that beer together, in Eppendorf, his hands kept on the table as if he were ready to leave, yet his voice calm, reassuring! The intervening years!

In the dream he let me off at a movie theater. Half the audience left early, booing, the other half applauding continuously. I too left early and now was looking for a telephone booth. I found one near a grocery store.

I dialed, Christian answered, my German came back to me "as if in a dream." We spoke about our hopes and fears; he explained that in the meantime he had joined the Socialist Party and had finally overcome his fear of dissecting corpses. For hours we talked; I expressed my shame at having accomplished, myself, in the same short period, so little.

"I'll pick you up in five minutes," he replied, once I had explained where I was.

I stood around in the parking lot, gently turning over pieces of gravel, one by one, with the toe of my shoe. After a while I thought that Christian had forgotten, the cars were rushing by, it had begun to drizzle; just as I was heading back inside he drove up in his shiny Volkswagen.

I opened the door and, as I was greeting him, awoke!

I felt shattered, as when in the public library I had come across the news, leafing through a literary magazine, that a friend had died. Had died!

I pushed back the dream, pushed back the covers, got out of bed, went to the kitchen, opened the shutters. It had been raining every day for days; now it was simply gray, the wind was blowing.

I turned on the radio.

I washed out the coffeepot, filled it with water, measured out the coffee, lit the burner.

I sponged off the table.

Then I just stood there, waiting—not really for anything—before awakening Françoise.

It was to an artist-friend that I spoke the other day about the upstairs hall window in the old house, about how recovering from polio I would stand there after morning kindergarten, after lunch in the kitchen with my mother, after my unvoiced pleas to play outside had gone unheard, after I had been guided to my bedroom for those convalescent naps which I almost never took. From my bedroom I would tiptoe back to the window as soon as I knew my mother herself had fallen asleep, in her bedroom just below mine, the sounds of doors and drawers opening and shutting, of blinds drawing, of mattress springs creaking. She would test the radio alarm; music and voices would blare; then there would be silence.

The upstairs hall window looked down on our tiny backyard squared on three sides by a privet hedge. Over the hedge and pin oak at the back of the yard was Nancy's backyard and house; next door to Nancy's was Steve's; Ruth and Ernie's hedge was visible over our garage and theirs; in the other direction a corner of Mrs. Shelley's garden and one of her elm trees could be seen. Behind Nancy's house rose the oak and elm trees of 49th Street and beyond.

Standing at the upstairs hall window, my arms crossed over the sill, I would watch Nancy and Steve and Diana and sometimes even the younger children, Jeannie and Jeff and Diana's brother Little Leonard, running around the yard or lined up by Nancy's mother into games.

Babies were strutted about; sand was piled; mud was molded. Down the slide came Dave. Goodwin sat, contented, in the leaves.

My mother kept the upstairs windows closed in fear of the cicada killers which hived under the roof on the north side. The air in the hallway was thus in all seasons damp and close—next to the hall window was the bathroom—, and the abiding moisture I would sense between my toes wriggling on the soft yarn of the new carpet. Ever so delicately I would pull open the patterned curtains; the curtain rings above would clink forward in fits and starts; but the window I never dared to push up. I would reach for the latch on the middle meeting rail, then press it between my thumb and forefinger, squeezing the brass lever which always felt cooler or warmer than I expected.

From such afternoons spent at the upstairs hall window came surely my propensity, to this day, to imagine myself apart, severed from, removed, to which should be added the enduring expectation of inevitable evanescence, of inevitable loss, Nancy and the others fleeing around the side of the house, vanishing....

"We played in the front yard after that," she explained as we walked to school the next morning.

But I had waited there at the window for the snowball fight to be battled back, the light snow falling crosswise, blown by the northwest wind I felt gusting against the back of my hand pressed against the freezing-wet window pane. I would stare at the leafless twigs and branches become a myriad of dessicated, upright sticks. Later that spring I peered into the dark, waxy greenness of the foliage below, already with the disorienting knowledge that the leaves and twigs and branches were growing thicker and denser and up and out all at once.

The images blend, overlap. The years slide together, past each other in opposite directions. Emotions once certainly disparate, at unexpected moments coalesce, Nancy's father Bud swinging his 5-iron, the summer he died, Gary Meert mowing the lawn thereafter for Doris Jean and sitting out late on the patio with Nancy's sister Susan. Susan's marriage years later to "Richard" or "Robert"—"or something like that," my mother would say—who three days after their honeymoon at Okoboji Lake ran his new motorcycle off Highway 6 into a telephone pole. Richard or Robert, about twenty-five years old.

Richard or Robert, Smitty, my mother.... From my upper window in Angers I look over the steep slate roofs, observe from afar the frenzy of the swallows. Sometimes they approach, race and dart about the chimneys. They cannot be watched for long: their frenzy dizzies. The thoughts they speed to me are dark.

I remove the swallows: the world must grow still.

There are moments when the world must grow still, with not a swallow or a breath of wind, just the bright summer sun on the slate gray roofs.

Paris, 1984 - Angers, 1988.

ABOUT THE AUTHOR

Since 1977 John Taylor has lived in France. A graduate of the University of Idaho and the University of Hamburg (Germany) where he studied mathematics, German literature, and philosophy, Taylor writes in English but has published his first two books in France. Taylor contributes reviews and articles to the *Times Literary Supplement, the San Francisco Chronicle, The Review of Contemporary Fiction* (of which he is a contributing editor), and other publications. He has lived in Greece and translated extensively from Greek modern writers, and appears as a frequent guest on French radio.